Also by Kaitlin Ward

Bleeding Earth

GIRL IN A BAD PLACE

Kaitlin Ward

Point

AN IMPRINT OF SCHOLASTIC INC.

All rights reserved. Published by Point, an imprint of Scholastic Inc., *Publishers since 1920*. SCHOLASTIC, POINT, and associated logos are trademarks and/or registered trademarks of Scholastic Inc.

The publisher does not have any control over and does not assume any responsibility for author or third-party websites or their content.

Library of Congress Cataloging-in-Publication Data Available

ISBN 978-1-338-10105-8

10 9 8 7 6 5 4 3 2 1   17 18 19 20 21 22

Printed in the U.S.A.   23

First edition, November 2017

Book design by Mary Claire Cruz

Photography © 2017 by Michael Frost

To Michelle Schusterman
The kind of friend who would rescue me from any
cult, and without whom this book would not exist

Summer

ONE

"Do you want to continue down a path of emptiness, or do you want to help bring order to this chaotic earth?"

When I hear this come out of the mouth of a girl no older than six, I stop walking. It's not the sort of thing you expect a kid that young to say—especially not at the mall on a Saturday afternoon. She's staring up at me earnestly with wild curls of brown hair pulled into two pigtails, and a tiny smudge of food on her cheek. I glance around, but there are no adults nearby who she might belong to.

"Are you lost?" My best friend, Cara, crouches so she's at eye level with the girl.

"No." The little girl smiles a precious, dimple-cheeked smile. "My mom's right over there. But I saw you walking and I thought you were the kind of people we need and I didn't want you to get away."

Cara and I exchange a look. This kid is . . . a touch creepy. "Let's get you back to your mom," Cara says uneasily.

We don't have to find the girl's mom, though; she finds us first, wild-eyed with panic. "Avalon! What have I *told* you about running off! Thank God."

The kid's mom is young—not as young as Cara and I, but young enough that even though I know I'm not supposed to judge . . . I'm judging a little. She's got bright green eyes and a thick braid of dark hair pulled over her shoulder. It's so long that it reaches the middle of her stomach. Her clothes are clean but her fingernails are filthy.

"Your little girl came up to us," Cara says. "We were about to help her find you, but she should really be careful about approaching strangers. It can be dangerous."

The woman's nostrils flare a bit. "I know that. Why do you think I was so worried?"

"She wasn't trying to judge your parenting." I step in. "She was just . . ."

My voice kinda fades out because I don't know where to go with my sentence. Cara doesn't mean to condescend, but she's pretty sensitive about the safety of kids after losing her younger sister in a car accident a couple years ago.

"I'm sorry," Cara says. "I didn't mean anything by it. I'm glad she's okay."

The woman lets out a breath and nods. "I shouldn't have snapped at you. You just get wound up when you turn around and your kid's not there, you know?"

"Mommy, I think they should come to the Haven," says the little girl—Avalon, I guess—tugging on her mother's shirt.

"Oh, sweetie, that's not what—"

But Avalon has turned back to us, enthusiastically. "We live at this place called the Haven. It's in the mountains and it's so pretty there. You should come. Please come?"

"It's a commune," the woman says quickly, almost apologetically. "Not anything weird. We just live off the land and stuff. We're not looking for more residents right now." The woman pauses and smiles at her daughter. "But Avalon is usually right about people, so if you wanted to come and visit, I think it'd be cool."

"A commune?" I don't know much about communes, but nature is gross. And filled with spiders. "I'm not sure—"

"Can you tell us more about it?" Cara interrupts. I blink at her. She doesn't notice my reaction, though, because her eyes are on the little girl.

"Sure! Come on, let's sit or something." The woman gestures toward a bench. "I'm Alexa, by the way."

"We're Cara and Mailee," says Cara as we join Alexa on the bench. Avalon squeezes between them.

"Well, about the Haven, there's not a lot to explain, really. We each have our own little houses. I mean, Avalon and I live together, but she's the only kid. So everyone else has their own house. Most of us are pretty young, like, early twenties. Firehorse is the oldest, he's forty-one. He's our founder." There's something reverent about the way she says his name.

"Firehorse?" It slips out before I can stop myself.

Alexa's expression cools. "Yes, Firehorse. And like I was saying, he's our founder. He's the reason the Haven exists. He created this beautiful, safe place for us to live, and he's *wonderful*."

"It sounds nice," Cara says, throwing me a sharp glance.

I keep my mouth shut. Maybe Alexa's into that guy or something, but don't tell me that's not a weird name.

"It is." Alexa smiles at Cara, and so does Avalon. "Firehorse owns the land, but it's surrounded by a bunch of preserves, mostly. It's so pretty. Just trees, a lake, nature. You kinda realize you don't need anything else once you're there, you know? Everything feels better, clearer. Body and mind. I love it. We're basically self-sustaining, and we work together at everything. You always know what needs to be done at any given time, you never have to feel purposeless. It's the best."

It doesn't sound bad, but it sounds *very* outdoorsy. Outdoors and I don't get along very well. My parents took my brother and me camping one time and it'll never happen again. Montana may be known for its wilderness, but it's easy enough to avoid nature if you're not a fan.

"So we could visit sometime, see what it's like?" Cara asks. Cara is about five percent more outdoorsy than I am, so I'm pretty surprised she's into this.

"Yes, absolutely. You'll have to call Firehorse and set up a time. To be courteous, you know? But it would be great if you visited, I think."

"So great!" Avalon pipes in.

"We'd love to."

I wish Cara had consulted me before using the word *we*, but . . . I don't know.

Here's the thing about Cara: She is right about everything. The only time she has ever been wrong was when we were ten years old and she thought that my fear of spiders could be cured by holding a tarantula at the pet store.

So, her one time being wrong, she was *super* wrong. But other than that, she's never led me astray. Which means that if she thinks it's a good idea to go visit some people we just met, at a commune in the woods with a leader named Firehorse, then it's probably a good idea.

Or, at least, not a *bad* idea.

So long as a spider doesn't try to touch me.

Cara gets Firehorse's contact details from Alexa and we say good-bye and go our separate ways. Once we're out of earshot, I turn to her.

"So . . . a commune?"

"I know," she says gleefully. "And a guy named *Firehorse*. If nothing else about this interests you, we have to at least see what a person named Firehorse looks like."

"Okay. You've got me there. Ten dollars says he has a red beard."

"That is *way* too obvious. I'll take that bet."

"I bet Jackson and Gavin are going to want to come with us."

"Probably. But I don't see why that'd be a problem."

I shrug. I'd rather they come, anyway. Safety in numbers. The commune sounds harmless, but like anywhere rural,

Montana has its fair share of off-the-grid weirdos. You never know.

Thinking about it, though, I do want to go. If I want a career as an actress—which I do—life experiences like this will be a big help.

"Well, that was quite a detour," I say. "We'd better get you that new planner you wanted. Otherwise we're *both* going to be disorganized, and that can only end in disaster. Can you even believe that this time next year we'll have *graduated*? This is our last summer as high schoolers."

"Yeah. It's crazy." Cara folds her arms, smile slipping.

I pretend not to notice the change in her mood. It's been like this since the last day of school; certain things seem to set her off, close her inside herself. I haven't figured out a pattern yet, and when I ask, she brushes me off. So I've stopped asking.

"Anyway," Cara says lightly, "we still have to clean your room, which has somehow turned into a *major* pigsty since I was in there last."

"My room is totally fine. Your standards are too high."

"Mailee. You can't see the floor."

This has been our friendship for the past decade. I am a whirlwind of chaos, and Cara is my rock. My parents love her because she cleans my room, and I love her because we are simultaneously total opposites and yet exactly the same.

We became best friends in second grade after she asked if she could clean my desk. I let her, and in return, I gave her a freshly sharpened pencil. It was a good trade; freshly sharpened pencils were a pretty serious commodity back then, and I prided myself on my ability to get the point *just right*. Our teacher gave us both gold stars that day for our cooperation, and we are major suckers for positive reinforcement.

The rest is history.

You can definitely see at least *some* of my floor.

Cara stands in the doorway, hands on her hips, and takes it all in like she's a general studying the map of a battlefield. My room is definitely cleaner than a battlefield.

"I don't understand how one person can make so much mess in so little time."

"I couldn't find the shirt I wanted, so I just pulled everything out."

She arches a blonde eyebrow at me. "Pulled?"

"Whatever, threw. Same difference."

She laughs. "You know, someday I'm going to visit you in your grown-up LA apartment and it's going to be all neat and organized, and I'm going to know that this was all worth it. Like how Michelangelo spent all that miserable time creating the Sistine Chapel, but look how nice it turned out."

"Well *that* was a little insulting."

"It was meant to be!" she teases. "And I'll give you one guess what I'm going to tell you to do now."

"Fold."

"You got it."

I hate folding. I hate putting clothes away. When they're all over my floor, I can see what I have. When they're tucked away in my drawer, I can never find anything. But my mom, and Cara, and society at large insist that clothing not be flung around my room like a decorative covering. Or as Cara puts it, like the first layer of a garbage dump.

While I fold, Cara flits around, taking care of the rest of my mess. It doesn't make me come off too well when others find out that my best friend literally cleans my room weekly, even if I do help. But she *likes* it. She likes making sure that everything looks just so, and she likes bossing people around. That's why she's worked behind the scenes on school plays for as long as I've been in them. We're going to rise to stardom together, me on-screen and her off. That's been the plan ever since she put it in the Book of Life Goals she started for us in middle school.

That plan has been the best thing that could've ever happened to me. It keeps me focused, gives me something to look forward to. Helps me concentrate on my future instead of whatever is in front of me right this very moment.

I've always been a big dreamer, but Cara's much better at taking dreams and combing through the practical aspects, bridging the gap between where I am now and where I want to end up.

She sweeps a handful of pencils and pens off my desk and deposits them in a pencil cup. Gently adjusts my emotions journal with a small smile. It's the one thing in my room that I always keep in the same spot. The one organized thing I did all on my own. It's where I record new emotions I experience, break them down and analyze them so I can use them to improve my performances when I'm acting.

My phone chirps its text message announcement, so I pause my folding to read it.

Still seeing you tonight? It's Gavin, my boyfriend.

Yup, I type back. And my room's gonna be clean and everything.

His reply comes within seconds. Nice. So I'll be able to sit down without crushing anything then.

The kissing-face emoji he includes at the end does *not* buy him forgiveness for his teasing. We've been going out for two months now, and it was definitely more than a month before I was willing to let him in my room when it wasn't within a day or two of a Cara cleaning. After that, I figured, if he's going to date me, he should probably know that this is what he's in for.

Though it wasn't like he had no warning. On our second date, I somehow managed to get chocolate ice cream on both our shirts without having actually dropped my cone. If this makes it sound like I'm adorably clumsy, I would like to be really clear: I am not. I'm actually not clumsy at all, I'm just straight up messy. It's not cute or endearing. It's the sort of thing that people love me in spite of, not because of, and I've known that for a long time.

"Who're you texting?" Cara asks in a singsong voice that tells me she already knows exactly who I'm texting.

"Gavin. He was just checking in about our plans for tonight."

"And what *are* your plans, if I may ask?" She straightens a pile of textbooks that was threatening to topple.

"Just dinner. Do you and Jackson want to come?" Cara has been dating her boyfriend for a little over a year now. Gavin and I are much newer, but thankfully, the boys get along pretty well.

"He's got some kind of family reunion thing today, so it's just me. You probably don't want the third wheel."

"You can still come if you want!"

"Mailee. I am not coming on your date without my boyfriend. All you do is gaze into each other's eyes like you're in a Disney movie or something."

"We do not." I throw a shirt at her.

"Hey! This is the opposite of folding."

"But folding is *so boring*!" I collapse dramatically onto my bed, limbs splayed.

"You are worse than a child." She yanks me back to my feet. "You know, even Harper wasn't this—"

She halts, voice catching in her throat. I chew on a fingernail, breath held, waiting to see if she wants to finish her sentence. She doesn't.

"You're thinking about her today, huh?" I ask. We both slump back on the bed, lying down on the folded clothes.

"Yeah. Today. Most days. That little girl at the mall just reminded me of her so much." She stares up at my ceiling, littered with glow-in-the-dark stars I put up years ago. "I know it's dumb, but seeing a little girl that age, with that spirit, it felt like . . . I don't know. Like I was meant to see that kid today. What are the odds, you know? That we'd run into this one little girl and get invited to the commune she lives in, and it's right before the anniversary of . . . you know."

She runs a hand absently down her arm. Cara was in the backseat, too, during the accident. But she was behind her mom on the driver's side, and the SUV that T-boned them hit the other side. Cara had some bruised ribs and a concussion, but was otherwise unhurt except for some slices where broken glass cut into her. Most of the scars have healed or faded, but there's a long one down her arm that'll never go away.

"Yeah. I get that." I pause, twisting a strand of brown hair around my finger, not entirely sure what to say next. It's been nearly two years since it happened, but this isn't the sort of thing you can just get over. The fallout hasn't stopped. Her parents used to be the kind of loving couple who were so into each other that it made everyone around them uncomfortable. You would have expected the tragedy to bring them closer together as a family, and at first it did. But Cara's father blames her mother for what happened, and her mother blames herself. Even though there was nothing she could've done about the drunk driver who blew through a red light. Cara's parents don't even sleep in the same room anymore, and I think Cara would be relieved if they'd just get divorced.

"I'm definitely all in if you want to go to that commune place," I say carefully. "But are you sure that's what you need? I mean, if you wanted to go back to therapy, I bet your mom would set it up."

"No, I don't want to do that. I'm fine, mostly. She doesn't need to worry that I'm, like, not coping. She's got enough to worry about as it is."

For the first several months after Harper's death, Cara and her mom both talked to a therapist every week. And then her mom decided that therapy had done all it could and she was capable of coping without it, so she stopped making appointments for either herself or Cara. Cara definitely wasn't ready to stop. It was helping her through more than just the loss, I think, even though she never said that to me.

"Okay." I find her hand and squeeze it. "I guess we're going to a commune, then."

She sits up and smiles at me. "Thank you."

"Do you think there's a special dress code? Do we have to wear skirts made of hemp? Give up shoes? Get dreadlocks?"

"I really doubt we'll have to do any of those things, Mailee. That girl and her daughter were both wearing shoes and they were both wearing jeans."

"Yeah, but maybe they were just trying to blend in with the outside world. Maybe when they're on the mountain they wear only furs."

Cara laughs. "Only furs? Your imagination is getting way too wild."

"My imagination is glorious."

"Sure, and so are your procrastination skills." She jumps up from my bed and yanks me along with her. "Don't think I've forgotten about all the clothes you're supposed to be folding."

"I'm suddenly feeling a deep weakness in both my arms. I think I've lost the ability to fold."

She picks up a pair of jeans and drops them on my head. "No more excuses. You have a date tonight; do you really want to have to cancel on Gavin because your room isn't clean yet?"

"You wouldn't." I clutch at my chest in faux horror.

"I would." She drops another pair of jeans on my head. One of the legs drapes over my eyes.

"Fine." I pluck the jeans away from my face and give her my best glare. "But I am going to remember that you black-mailed me."

She grins and goes back to organizing my desk. "You say that every week."

TWO

Two days later, we are on our way to the commune. The Haven. As we predicted, our boyfriends wanted to come, too, and Gavin volunteered to drive us in his truck. Given the quality of the roads we have to take to get there, that's both a great and a horrible thing. It'll be harder for this truck to get stuck in a muddy rut, but it's also been a bit of a rough ride. And part of me absolutely can't believe we're doing this.

Cara called the Firehorse guy who runs this place. I listened on speakerphone while she talked to him. It was all a load of major hippie crap. Nothing against hippies at all, just there's a level at which you take things too far, and Firehorse is way past that level. He actually said stuff like, "I would delight in welcoming you to our serene little corner of nature." Let me tell you, serene is not how I feel when I'm in nature, but Cara was way into the whole thing, and it's pretty much all she's been excited about yet this summer, so here we are.

And Firehorse wasn't lying. We are thoroughly ensconced in nature. What started out as a paved road has turned into two rutted, barely visible tracks as we've gone deeper into the wild. The closer the tree branches get to the sides of Gavin's truck, the more apprehensive I become. But I'm excited, too. I've never been to one of these off-the-grid places before, and I've always been curious. There's something comforting about the whole concept. Constructing a civilization for yourself outside of society where you all harmoniously coexist and don't have to worry about stressful stuff like money and college and careers.

But if I become a famous actress, I won't have to worry about those things, either, and I also won't have to sleep where surprise contact with spiders is a real and ever-present danger.

"Did you know this place was so far out here?" Jackson asks Cara. And he does not use a nice tone.

"It's not *that* far," Cara replies. She's pretending to inspect the ends of her honey-blonde hair, but she catches my gaze in the rearview mirror and in that fraction of a second, we have a transmission that doesn't require words or even a change in expression. The message is: *No, neither of us had any idea we were going this far into nowhere.*

"It's been about an hour since we left Mailee's house," says Gavin. "I'm sure we'll be there soon. The going's just slow what with the road quality and all."

Jackson slumps down in his seat. It's a little dramatic in my opinion, and if anyone knows dramatic, it's me. He looks ridiculous back there anyway; Gavin's truck doesn't have a full-sized cab. The seats in the back face each other, folding out from the sides below the back windows. Jackson's too big, really, to fit back there, but I'm the girlfriend so I get the front. Once Jackson slumps, Cara is completely squished into her corner.

The ruts in the path grow even deeper and muckier, and the grass in the middle even taller. Pine needles brush the top of the windshield and it's making me claustrophobic. I hope Cara and I haven't gotten ourselves into a situation where some human-monster hybrid has placed rusted barbed wire across the road and we're going to get a flat tire and then be eaten alive in the woods. Brunettes tend to fare better than blondes in horror movies, so maybe I'd survive. Though my sense of direction is less than zero, so I probably shouldn't bank on my hair color to save me.

I glance down at my clothes and realize that if we *do* get stuck, even for non-horror-movie reasons, I am so not equipped to walk too far. The underbrush surrounding the road is thick and brambly. The road itself such a mess. And I'm wearing flip-flops, a pair of tight jeans, and a white tank top. What was I thinking? Well, I know exactly what I was thinking. It's the same thing I was thinking when I spent a half hour this morning straightening my hair even though it's already pretty straight on its own. And when I painted on my makeup with extra care, lined my gray eyes until they brightened. And when I stared at myself in the mirror trying to decide if these pants make me look like I actually have a butt or if there's no getting away from the fact that I'm a "stick," as I've been called many times.

It's because Gavin is here, and I would rather look as pretty as possible when he's nearby, even if it's impractical.

The trees edge even closer together, and the road—if I can call it that—is getting boggy. When I glance at Gavin, the muscles in his chiseled jaw are working. Gavin is a saint. If he agrees to go along with something, even if he warned me beforehand that he thinks it's a bad idea, he never rubs it in my face when he's proven right. But I can tell, right now, he's wishing he hadn't agreed to this. His clenched jaw says, *I told you so I told you so why don't you ever listen to me Mailee* while his mouth stays silent. A degree of self-control I will never obtain even if I live to be one thousand years old.

"Maybe we should try to back up," I say tentatively as branches grope at the truck from all angles and the tires whine, fighting for grip in the mud. "Maybe I got it wrong when I mapped this out."

"We'd have to back up the whole way out," Gavin says. "There's nowhere to turn around. So let's call that a last resort. You know we're going the right way. There's no other way we could have gone. It's probably just that people don't drive out here that often. I'm sure we're almost—"

He stops because we've emerged into a big clearing. There are a couple cars parked at the far side of the clearing, and beyond them are some metal shacks. The glistening surface of a lake is visible in the background. If they replaced the metal shacks with log cabins, this is the sort of picture they'd put in a Montana brochure to convince people to move here. It's gorgeous.

"I knew we'd find it!" Cara claps her hands together in glee.

"Where should I park?" Gavin asks. "Over by those other cars?"

"Wherever," I say, "so long as I don't have to walk through too much tall grass."

Tall grass in the summer houses ticks, and ticks are even worse than spiders. Spiders are creepy, but at least they serve a purpose. Ticks serve no purpose other than being disgusting and spreading diseases. They should have been thrown off the ark. After being set on fire to make sure they were really dead.

"I'll carry you," Gavin says, and he winks at me.

I feel myself blush. It's always noticeable when I blush because I'm so pale, and it's embarrassing, but Gavin seems to find it cute. Cara says we're in the "infatuation phase" and that eventually we'll stop finding everything about each other so adorable, but I don't know. It's been two months and I still melt into a puddle every time he touches me. Looks at me. Exists in my general vicinity.

Gavin drives slowly across the rock-strewn field, parking near the other cars. Gavin's truck isn't anything fancy; his parents bought it for him when he turned sixteen, and it's close to a decade old with well over a hundred thousand miles on it. But these other vehicles make it look high-end. Rust corrodes holes like the spots of a Holstein cow, and both are blanketed in dried-up layers of old pine needles.

There's another vehicle, though, parked next to one of the shacks, that's a whole lot nicer. A big, sleek SUV. The rusty cars make more sense. Who needs them, right, after you move to a self-sufficient commune? Though, I guess, Alexa had to get into town somehow.

A man emerges from the shack beside the SUV as Gavin shuts off his truck. I know immediately, without doubt, that this person is Firehorse. He has that look. I mean, to take on a name like that, you'd have to be pretty serious about yourself. He swaggers closer to us with a glowing smile. He's got bright blue eyes and shoulder-length gray-peppered brown hair.

He wears a flannel shirt partway open, exposing more chest hair than I want to see, a dreamcatcher necklace, and sun-leathered skin. And he tucks the flannel shirt into Wrangler jeans, completing the look with a pair of cowboy boots. The boots are pretty fancy, not the sort of thing you'd picture some-one wearing to be comfortable in nature. They don't have any scuffs, and look like they're made of real leather. Like what kids at my school wear when they want to look all rugged but never actually leave our suburbs. I picture the boots lined up in Gavin's mudroom, the ones reserved for work on his family's ranch, and these are basically the exact opposite.

I tear my gaze from the boots, back up to Firehorse's face. Alexa said he was forty-one. If that's true, then he's a cautionary tale about spending too much time outdoors without sunscreen. He's kind of good-looking, though, I realize with an embarrassed sensation in my gut. For someone who's barely younger than my parents, anyway.

"Um, I guess we should get out?" Cara says. She doesn't sound as nervous as I suddenly feel. "And if that's Firehorse, you owe me, Mailee."

Crap. No red beard. "I didn't forget."

I exchange a glance with Gavin and I can tell he is Not Having This. But we're here, so we might as well see what the commune is about, right? So, with confidence, I open my door and step out. The others follow my example.

"Welcome!" Firehorse says. His voice is gravelly and pleasant, the kind you could listen to for hours. He reaches out and grasps my hand with both of his. His palms are surprisingly smooth for someone who lives in the woods. "You must be the Cara I spoke with over the phone?"

"No," I say quickly. Beside me, Cara frowns. "I'm Mailee."

"My mistake!" He chuckles embarrassedly. "You just have the face of a Cara, I guess."

The face of a Cara. What is that, even?

He gives my hand a final pat and moves on to the actual Cara. I want to ask what name she has the face of, but I don't have the guts.

Firehorse gives Cara the same two-handed grasp greeting as he gave me, and adds a shoulder squeeze. For Gavin, he downgrades to a regular old handshake. Maybe he can tell from the look on Gavin's face that the complete hand envelopment might be a little too much.

"I wasn't expecting four of you," Firehorse says, just as he's letting go of Gavin's hand. His smile falters for the briefest moment. "Alexa had only mentioned two."

"I'm sorry," Cara says quickly. "I should have asked on the phone. I didn't think it would be a problem."

"No, no. The more, the better," says Firehorse, turning to Jackson. Only I don't think he really feels like more is better. I think he's secretly annoyed.

Jackson gets the coolest reception by far. A curt nod and a thin-lipped smile. To Firehorse's credit, Jackson's scowl is so sharp it could cut glass. But I'm still surprised. I assumed Firehorse was so fake, he'd be nice to anyone, no matter what attitude they radiate. Maybe he's realer than I thought.

"So tell me," says Firehorse, shepherding us toward what appears to be the main part of the camp. "What brings the four of you here? And I don't mean literally. I know you came because you met Alexa and Avalon, and I know that you were transported here in a truck. But what was it, in your spirits, that moved you to come?"

I get that feeling like when you're in English class and you haven't done the reading and the teacher starts asking questions. When you're just hoping they can't sense your fear and won't call on you. I don't know why I'm here. I don't think that he'll appreciate *communes are kinda weird and I wanted to see one* as my answer. Luckily, Cara rescues me.

"Alexa and Avalon made it all sound so nice," she says. "Everyone has a purpose here. You know what you're going to do each day, and you just do it. And you're part of something. You're a community."

It's such a perfectly Cara answer, I can't help but smile. Of course she would love the organization and planning and everything having a place. I've been her biggest organizational project for years, but maybe she's thinking of expanding her efforts. Then again, I am basically the Everest of organizational projects. It's going to be a while before she conquers me.

"And you?" Firehorse turns his electric-blue eyes toward me. Uh-oh. I've been called on.

"Um. I guess I came because I trust Cara's judgment and if she wants to do something or go somewhere, it always turns out great."

"And I think I can speak for Gavin and myself both," Jackson says, "that we came because our girlfriends wanted us to."

Firehorse chuckles. "That is as good a reason as any. We, as men, need to make sure that women feel their opinions are just as valued."

I decide to give him the benefit of the doubt on that and assume he phrased badly. Otherwise, it's pretty insulting.

"Can I ask a question?" Cara says timidly.

"Of course." Firehorse beams at her.

"Well . . . where is everyone? There are others who live here besides Avalon and Alexa, right?"

"Oh yes, of course there are others! There are about two dozen of us. We have a small logging camp nearby, up in the trees. That's where the rest of the group is right now, harvesting some trees for firewood. I stayed behind because I knew you were coming; the others will be back in a bit. It's nice to have visitors, but our schedule's important, too, I hope you understand."

It's a little awkward, to be honest. A lot more pressure to make a good impression when there's a single person than when you're mixed nicely into a crowd. And there's something about Firehorse that makes me want to be impressive.

"You're all in high school?" Firehorse asks. He leans forward while he speaks, like he's actually interested, not just asking to be polite.

"We're all going to be seniors this fall," I say proudly. I'm never going to get tired of telling people I'm a senior. It's felt like it would never come. But here I am, finally, standing in the doorway of my final year of high school.

Cara's expression sours. I'm starting to think she isn't excited about our senior year. Her attitude stomps on the embers of my excitement. Firehorse's gaze rests on her frown. He doesn't know us at all, but he senses it, too.

"Senior year is a very exciting time," he says with a smile. "And a stressful time. Lots of change."

I shrug. The real time of change isn't till the end of next summer, when we all go off to college. I'm not thinking about that yet. About how Cara and I might end up in different places, how Gavin plans to go to college locally and take over his dad's ranch. That's the stuff that makes my stomach hurt. Senior year itself is joy. It's having a chance at the lead role in school plays. It's college applications. It's knowing I'm on the brink of adulthood, finally.

"Yeah," Cara says the word as a sigh. "Lots of change, for sure."

I don't want to argue here in front of Firehorse, so I say nothing and gaze around at the scenery instead.

The terrain around the Haven is rocky and uneven. It's nestled in a valley; when I mapped out how to get here, the path-like road we just drove along looked like God took a finger and dragged a line between two steep mountains and then made a thumbprint at the end. We're standing in the thumbprint. And for a place that's self-sustaining, it's not the best-looking farmland. There's no livestock or crops, that I can see. Where we stand now, the ground has been mostly cleared of rocks. It's smooth and well-worn with footpaths. A giant fire pit sits at the center of everything, and about fifteen metal shacks and something that looks suspiciously like an outhouse. Now, when I say these shacks are made of metal, I mean entirely metal. Roof, sides, everything. They're not particularly big, either, but they look livable, I guess. At least from the outside.

There's a half-enclosed food preparation area and a big garden off to the side of everything. The lake shimmers peacefully in the background, with several kayaks tied to a rickety wooden dock.

None of this is my thing. I am an indoors girl. I like plumbing and hot water and places where insects and wildlife are unlikely to accost me. I like trying new things with makeup and practicing facial expressions in the mirror and dreaming about the day when I move to California and land my first movie role. But something about it is very cozy and homelike. Maybe I'm crazy. I'm definitely crazy. I would never in a million years live here. But I don't feel sad for the people who do, I guess is what I'm saying.

Gavin definitely does not feel the same way. His facial expression gives an illusion of pleasantness, but knowing him as well as I do, I can tell that he wants nothing more than to get the hell out of here. Jackson doesn't look like he's *loving* the place, but he's definitely more interested than Gavin.

"So can you tell us how it works?" he asks Firehorse. "Living here?"

"Certainly!" Firehorse shepherds us toward benches made out of halved trees that surround the fire pit. "It's simple, really. Everyone at the Haven understands that our world is corrupt and ready to implode, and that the best thing we can do for ourselves is to make our own community, to reject the society we don't want to emulate. We need to be cleansed from the oppressions of society. Need to let our bodies and minds recover from the toxins. Our ancestors lived off the land, and we can do it, too."

"What about these buildings?" Gavin gestures to one of the metal shacks. "Making something out of metal isn't exactly 'living off the land.'"

Firehorse's beaming smile doesn't even falter. He's definitely in his element, explaining all this to us. "No, these are not from the land. They had been discarded in our wilderness, and we repurposed them. Isn't that better than leaving them where they were, to pollute the environment?" He pauses for a small chuckle. "But I know some of these issues are hard to grasp, when schools are only teaching you the government's agenda these days."

A defensive burn settles into my stomach. We're not only learning the government's agenda. I know plenty of things.

"Our school isn't teaching us any kind of agenda," says Jackson, echoing my thoughts. "They're teaching us facts."

"Facts can be spun in all sorts of ways," Firehorse says. His tone is absent, almost bored, like he's had this conversation with people a million times and he's so over it. "The government has been pushing its version of the truth for so long, people no longer know the reality. Everyone's been so propagandized that it's hard to question what we've been told."

Jackson looks blown away by this. I'm not nearly as certain. Not that I don't understand his point. I know that there are layers upon layers we don't dig into about wars and civil rights and the founding of our nation and everything in history, basically. But it sounds to me like what Firehorse is implying is deeper than revisionist history, and on that front, I'm just not sure.

"Where do you get your meat and stuff?" Cara asks. "Do you hunt?"

"We don't eat meat. We're all vegans here," says Firehorse.

Uh-oh. I reach reassuringly for Gavin's hand. His parents' ranch is populated with beef cattle; he is *not* a fan of veganism.

"So . . . no ice cream?" Cara's eyes widen.

Firehorse chuckles. "No, but where do you think we'd keep the ice cream anyway?"

"That's fair." Cara grins.

"I have to ask about your name," I say, because I've wanted to ask since the moment Alexa said it, and if I hold in the question any longer, I'll explode.

Firehorse smiles, which is a relief. I feared he'd be defensive like Alexa. "If I had a nickel for every time I heard that question. I know it's a unique name, but the name I was given at birth was so plain, I wanted something memorable." He pauses for a long moment. "I wanted something no one who heard of me would ever forget."

"Mission accomplished," says Cara approvingly.

Suddenly, Firehorse's eyes flicker to something above my head. My spine tingles with that sensation you get when it feels like someone's right behind you, reaching out . . .

I turn. No one's there, of course. But people are streaming down the steep hillside. Quite a few of them. It's as if they appeared out of nowhere. They move slowly, carefully, across the uneven terrain, like a shambling zombie militia.

"Are those the other members?" I ask. It's a dumb question, because obviously.

Firehorse nods and continues to watch them make their way closer with a deep fondness in his eye. If nothing else, this guy is definitely way into the commune and all its members. That much, anyone could see.

"Those are my Colonists," he says proudly.

As the others approach the camp, they surround us wordlessly. The smell of body odor is strong, which I guess is to be expected after a whole group of people has been out working in the sun on a hot day. They're all dirt-streaked and glistening, and many of them carry things like saws and axes. Most of them are women. I only see four guys. Everyone's face is serious. Given how smiley Firehorse is, I expected them all to be a little friendlier.

Firehorse stands and holds out his arms in a sweeping motion. "We have guests!" he says. "Let us greet them warmly, please."

The serious expressions disappear, and choruses of "Welcome!" echo from all around us. It actually makes my skin crawl a little. Just the hive-mindedness of everyone welcoming us almost in unison, and on command.

I accidentally meet the gaze of one of the boys. He can't be much older than I am, and his face hasn't transformed like everyone else's has. He wears a permascowl, much like the expression Jackson had when we first got here, before he decided he was kinda interested. It takes a while for the boy to tear his eyes away from me, and when he does, it's to look down at his ax. He brushes his thumb across the sharp edge, almost lovingly, and then walks away, toward one of the shacks.

Only when he's gone inside and shut the door behind him do I realize that I've basically been staring unrelentingly at some random guy for a full minute with my boyfriend sitting right beside me. My boyfriend who definitely noticed the staring. He's frowning at me.

"I think we need to head out," he says.

"But we just got here!" Cara protests. "And everyone else just got here, too."

"Yes, there's no need to depart yet!" Firehorse exclaims. "Stay, meet everyone!"

Gavin is beyond uncomfortable, but Cara is so into this. My stomach hurts a little, torn between the wishes of two people I both want happy. "Just another hour," I tell Gavin.

"Fine," he says thinly.

But when Cara and Jackson get up to mingle with all the new arrivals, Gavin doesn't follow. He wanders away, back toward his truck. I'm torn again. I want to talk to these people, find out what it's like to live someplace like this. When am I going to get an opportunity again? But I also feel like Gavin's mad at me, and I don't want him to be mad at me. So I follow him.

"I'm sorry," I say, when we're out of earshot of everyone else. "I know you want to leave, but Cara has been so . . . it's nice to see her interested in something."

"I know. It's fine, really." His tone belies his words. "I just think this place is kinda creepy."

"Are you maybe being a little hard on them because they're vegans?"

His mouth twists, fighting a smile. "No."

I tilt my head.

"Okay, maybe." He loses the fight against his smile and kisses me. "One more hour, though, that's all I've got in me. That guy calls them *Colonists*. And you saw his necklace, right?"

"I saw."

Gavin's family doesn't live on the reservation—which is quite a ways north of us—but they are tribally enrolled Blackfeet. His heritage matters to him, and he's taught me a lot about cultural appropriation. It's been really eye-opening. It's crazy how little thought we give things sometimes, just because they don't affect us directly. Some particular least-favorites for Gavin include: Native American Halloween costumes (especially the "sexy" ones), anything dreamcatcher-related (especially because they're so mass-produced and improperly attributed these days), and headdresses on hipsters.

We return together to the group. I spot Alexa with a couple other people, down near the water. But we don't head toward them, we head toward Cara and Jackson, who are in the food preparation area with a few girls, including little Avalon. It's a three-sided wooden structure with a dirt floor. There's a big, long table that takes up most of it, with knives and silverware and other utensils scattered all over. Giant cabinets take up the whole back wall.

Cara is chopping up a very robust-looking bell pepper. I'm suspicious about whether this thing was homegrown. Maybe I'm not outdoorsy, but I've seen my mom's vegetable garden, and it's never produced anything like that pepper.

"Where do you guys plant all of this?" I ask.

One of the girls looks up at me. She's slicing potatoes. "Didn't you see it? The garden's pretty big. Most of it's behind this building."

Gavin and I both go look. I *had* noticed the garden before, but hadn't seen how far it extended. It's expansive, with nice, healthy-looking plants. But big enough to sustain all of these people through all the seasons? All the way through a Montana winter? I realize that I have no idea how you'd survive the winter while living off the land, especially without meat. But I'm also not a survival expert.

"Do you kind of get the feeling this living off the land thing is a load of crap?" Gavin asks me quietly.

A throat clears behind us, and we jump around. Firehorse is standing there. Well, this is awkward.

"Our garden sustains us just fine," says Firehorse with an unhappy gleam in his eye. "And it is not our only source of food. We do a lot of foraging. And, young man, I understand that you came here for your girlfriend's sake, but we do not need this kind of negative energy here. Your skepticism is exactly the sort of thing we all came to the Haven to elude."

"I'm sorry if you feel I'm being negative," says Gavin tightly. "But I think the both of us are going to just have to accept that we have some philosophical differences."

"Your close-mindedness is very unfortunate," says Firehorse. "Don't be angry with me for caring about our planet. I cannot make anyone believe. You have to come to it on your own. But this might help."

He hands us each a business card. They're blank except for the address of some website, handwritten in neat, even lettering.

"What's this?" I ask. I'm not the one who was rude, but I feel guilty nonetheless. Firehorse seems so nice—if a bit quirky—and I don't want his feelings hurt.

"It's my website," Firehorse says. "I don't maintain it anymore, now that I live here, but the information is still accurate. It explains a lot about who we are and why we do this. And it summarizes the problems I have with our current world. You don't have to look at it if you don't want to, but I would hate to think that you were too set in your ways even at this young age to open yourselves up to a new and well-researched viewpoint."

I put the business card in my pocket, a little embarrassed by how unpleasant Gavin's being. It's usually me who blurts out all my thoughts, not him.

"We'll definitely look at it," I say, even though it's more likely the card will end up in the wash and the ink will bleed out of it and I'll never think of it again after that.

I promised Cara we'd stay another hour, so we do stay another hour, but it's pretty awkward after Gavin and Firehorse's confrontation. Cara and Jackson get into the thick of things—cutting up and roasting vegetables, learning how to make bread, chopping firewood—and I try to be involved, too, but I feel like no one wants me here anymore. Because I'm Gavin's girlfriend, we are obviously the same person with all the same thoughts and I can't possibly want to help them with anything if he doesn't. I'm tempted to go join Gavin, who's sitting alone on the dock with his toes in the water.

But then Alexa approaches me.

"Everyone gets into their routine," she says. "We're not used to having new people, and I don't think anyone quite knows what to do with *this many* new people, either. But here, let me show you something."

I follow her, curious. She takes me to the other side of the encampment, where there's a really big, metal trapdoor in the ground. It has a logo carved into its surface. The letter *H* with a circle around it, and the word *verum* running sideways up the left side of the letter. I'm pretty sure that means *truth* in Latin. Alexa lifts it open. Inside, a ladder leads down into the earth.

Um. No way.

Alexa must sense my apprehension, because she points to the underside of the trapdoor. "Don't worry, it has a safety release! We can't get locked in."

She starts down the ladder, and I don't want to be a wimp, so I follow. We leave the trapdoor open, and sunlight flows in through the opening. The walls are rock, and the floor is dirt. I try not to think about spiders or earwigs or other crawling things.

"This is our root cellar. We store preserves and roots and beans and all kinds of stuff down here."

She gestures, and I see what she's talking about. Once we get away from the entrance, there are shelves everywhere. Jars of preserves, labeled containers.

"And *this*"—she goes on as she opens another trapdoor, one made of wood this time, and points—"is where we put the stuff that needs to be kept extra cold. It's an underground freezer. Reach your hand down and feel the temperature."

I obey, and I'm surprised how chilly the air is. "Wow. This is actually pretty neat."

She smiles. "I thought you might think so. I know you probably had an idea of what this place was going to be. Maybe a part of you came here with the intent of tearing apart everything about our commune, even if it was subconsciously. But we really do live off the land as much as possible. Firehorse is pretty intense. He can be a lot to get used to at first, but he just has so much knowledge. And people are still always ignoring what he has to say. He gets really passionate."

"I'm so sorry if I've made you feel judged," I tell her. "I actually think he seems really nice. And this place is very beautiful. My boyfriend just expected something different, I think."

"People usually do. But in the end, I guess they'll see, won't they?"

"Yeah. I guess they—"

I stop, because I notice something about the trapdoor to the freezer. Its exposed underside is scratched up. Like it's been clawed at by desperate fingernails.

"What's the matter?" Alexa asks.

"Nothing, sorry. I thought I saw a spider. I'm really glad you showed me this, but can we get out of here? Bugs creep me out."

"Sure, of course." She closes the trapdoor, and I suppress a shudder. It's probably my imagination. It gets away from me sometimes. Okay, it gets away from me a lot. I am a major worst-case imaginer.

She stares at me for a moment, biting her lip. "You're wondering about the scratches."

My stomach clenches, and I try to look casual as I step out of easy reach.

"It's okay," she says. "I wasn't going to bring it up because it was a terrible tragedy, but since you noticed . . ."

I swallow, but the dryness in my throat doesn't disappear.

"One of our members . . . she had an accident down there."

"She got trapped?" I ask, my voice barely a whisper.

Alexa nods.

"Is she okay?"

Hesitation. "No."

Oh God. I try to imagine. You're trapped in a claustrophobic space, so desperate that you dig at a wooden trapdoor hard enough that it looks like a bear got to it. Getting colder and colder until you just . . . die.

"This door doesn't have one of those safety releases on it?"

"It didn't." Alexa frowns down at the door. "Firehorse had one put on right after. We're only supposed to come down here in pairs, you know? That seemed like precaution enough. But precautions only work if everyone follows the rules. It was hard on all of us, after."

Rules or not, I would never in a million years trust anyone, not even Gavin, not even Cara or my brother or my parents, enough to set foot in that freezer. I don't think I'd set foot in there even *with* the safety release.

"I can imagine," I say softly. "I'm so sorry."

I know ghosts aren't real and all that, but suddenly I feel a chill, like the spirit of the dead girl is here, haunting the cellar, begging for justice.

Did they really not notice her absence for hours? No one heard her scream or anything? "It was very tragic," says Alexa, "but it was also . . . I mean, I don't want to speak ill of the dead, but she should have been more careful. It was so preventable. People need to take our supplies seriously, and not—she shouldn't have come here alone. And she'd still be with us."

The shock I feel at her words must be plain on my face, because she rushes on, "Not that I'm saying she deserved to die! I'm just saying, I wish she'd known better, hadn't made such a foolish mistake."

"Of course, yeah. That's really sad."

Alexa's jaw tightens. "It was a very difficult time for us. Anyway, I'm sorry. I didn't mean to make this about a dark thing, and I don't want you to think of us as careless. Opal was a friend, and I miss her every day."

I can relate to that. I'm almost compelled to tell her about Harper, but I try to always let Cara be the one to tell new people about her family history. Even though thinking about Harper, remembering her sweet little face, is hard for me, too. I spent half my childhood bickering with my older brother and begging my parents for a little sister. Harper was born when Cara and I were nine, and to me, my friend having a little sister felt like the next best thing.

Harper and the girl in this root cellar—both were tragic accidents. It's easy to sweep in from outside the situation and try to assign blame, but I wasn't here. I don't know what every-one was doing when this girl got trapped, how far away they might have been at the time.

And I don't know what to say, so I reach out and give Alexa's forearm a comforting squeeze.

"Thank you." She smiles tremblingly. "Ugh, I can't believe I turned your tour of the grounds into such a mess. Let's just get back up into the sunlight."

"It's totally fine. I'm glad you told me."

But I can be understanding and creeped out at the same time, and I make sure I'm the first one up the ladder. She definitely notices, but it doesn't seem to bother her.

Cara and the guys and I leave shortly after that. I can't stop thinking about the scratched-up trapdoor, how sad it is. I can't decide if I should tell everyone or not. Cara's in such a good mood, and she's easily triggered by tragedy. I'll wait, I decide, and tell Gavin later, when Cara's not nearby.

"That was pretty fun, right?" Cara says as we're driving back along the mountain path.

I exchange a glance with Gavin, and smile knowingly. "It had its moments," I say.

"Not as bad as I expected," adds Jackson, which is pretty high praise, coming from him.

"I'd rather castrate a bull by myself than go back," says Gavin.

All of us laugh at that.

THREE

Of all the many facets of nature Montana offers, water is the kind I like best. There's a lake about a ten-minute drive from my house with a great public beach. And an even better thing about the lake is that Jackson's family owns a lakefront camp there. Since Cara's been dating him, I've been upgraded from public beach to private beach. Way fewer small, screaming children.

It's a million degrees out today, so a bunch of us are meeting at Jackson's camp to keep ourselves from melting. Gavin's picking me up, and I'm waiting impatiently in the kitchen with my dad. My mom is abysmal at cooking, but she gets home from work earlier than he does, so he spends much of his Sundays preparing meals and writing explicit cooking instructions so that Mom doesn't burn the house down (as she almost did one time). And whenever he can catch me, Dad ropes me into watching him, because he says he'd like me to be able to at least cook passably enough that I won't poison myself when I'm off on my own.

My dad is a major goofball and a huge dork. In an endearing way, usually. But right now he's finding it super hilarious to have a puppet show with a chicken and an oven mitt, and I would rather be in the dark about the unsanitary things he does with the food I eat.

So I'm relieved when I hear the rumble of Gavin's beat-up truck outside. "I'll be back in time for dinner!" I yell as I run for the door.

"Have fun!"

He doesn't ask where I'm going. My parents only care about that stuff if it's an overnight thing. They do the kind of parenting that people are now calling "free-range." I've always been trustworthy, and until I'm not, there's no reason for them to worry. Cara jokes that if I ever decide to do something untrustworthy, I'd better make it really good.

So far, nothing worthy's come up.

Gavin smiles at me when I hop into his truck. Half of me would love to skip out on my friends and spend the day just the two of us. The other half of me is already sweaty from the five seconds I've been outside and can't wait to go to the beach. There's a shirt and some towels strewn haphazardly across the backseat of the truck, but Gavin's wearing only his swim trunks right now. Given that we're on our way to the beach, I obviously knew I'd be seeing him without his shirt today, but I wasn't expecting it already. I feel a little thrown off. There's something uncomfortably vulnerable about liking someone as much as I like Gavin. About knowing you've opened your heart to the chance for complete devastation.

But you can't live in a world where you cocoon yourself from feelings. At least, I can't.

I like to experience every emotion as intensely as I can. I like to dissect them, analyze them, memorize every aspect. Take notes on them in my emotions journal. The deeper my understanding of every emotion possible, the better actress I'll be. It's not memorizing lines that's the hard part. Not saying the words or going through the motions. It's feeling what your character feels, and showing it to the audience. Making it real.

I've had other boyfriends before, but none of them ever made things feel *real* quite like Gavin does.

Before he starts driving, Gavin leans over to give me a kiss. "You look pretty," he says.

I roll my eyes. I'm not wearing any makeup and my hair's in a messy bun, because there's zero point in trying to look hot when you're about to go jump into water. But I did spend a while deciding what shorts and tank top to wear over my bathing suit.

Gavin backs his truck out of my driveway onto the road. "You do," he insists.

"And so do you."

"Thanks. Took me a long time to style my hair." He pats the top of his head gingerly, as though he actually has styled hair. It's just regular boy hair, cropped short. Barely worth even running a comb through (which I doubt he did).

Gavin doesn't need to be a high-maintenance guy anyway. He's got dark hair, dark eyes, and long lashes. He's several inches taller than me and he's lean but muscular. He does a lot of manual labor on his family's ranch, and let me tell you, it has paid off.

I reach out and take his hand. He smiles at me. His teeth are just crooked enough not to count as perfect, but not so crooked that he ever had to get braces. When he smiles at me like that, I can't help but feel like this is going to be my best summer so far.

Jackson and Cara are already at the camp somewhere when we arrive. Jackson's impractical two-door sedan sits in the driveway of the camp. Gavin pulls his truck in behind it. My friend Samantha and her girlfriend, Margaret, pull in just as Gavin and I are getting out, and behind them is a carful of Jackson's friends.

Samantha greets me with an enthusiastic hug. I haven't seen her since school ended a couple weeks ago. Margaret's greeting is a shy wave. They've only been dating about as long as Gavin and I have, so Margaret and I don't really know each other that well yet.

"It is ridiculously hot today." Samantha plucks at the tank top she wears over her bathing suit.

"I'm sweating out of my skin," I say. "Let's get in the water."

Jackson's friends come with us, but they don't really say anything. They're all super into sports and we don't have that much in common. Gavin gets along with them fine, but he has his own group of friends, so I don't think he's bonded that much with these guys.

Jackson's family owns the end unit on a strip of close-packed camps. It's reached by stairs cut into a steep hill down from where we parked, and it's got tan siding and big windows. Nothing too exciting about it; your typical inherited-from-grandparents beach property. It felt weird coming here last summer, but I've been enough times now that I'm not uncomfortable anymore.

Inside the house, big sliding glass doors lead out to a deck. We all flow out back, where Cara sits on the beach, facing the water, and Jackson wrestles pool floats out of the storage underneath the deck.

Ten minutes later, I'm on one of those pool floats. Cara, Sam, Margaret, and I have wound a water-skiing rope through the arms of our floats and turned ourselves into an island. We tied the end of the rope around a tree on shore so we can't be carried out too far by the waves. The boys are all sitting on the deck, which, in my opinion, defeats the purpose of coming to the beach. They're cooking us burgers, though, so I can't complain.

"Are you guys getting excited for theater camp?" Sam asks.

"Yes! I'm so excited that I even wrote out a list of all the stuff I need to get before we go," I tell her, taking a sip from the cup of lemonade I stowed precariously into the float's cup holder.

"You made a list?" Cara's tone is disbelieving.

"With little boxes next to each item and everything. So I can check them off." I grin at her. "You've done good work on me."

"I guess so." She unscrews the cap from her bottle of water but doesn't drink.

"If Mailee made a list," says Samantha, "then you're probably already packed, huh, Cara?"

Now Cara drinks from her water. Slowly. She screws the cap back on just as slowly, then sweeps her eyes across the three of us. "I'm actually not going."

My stomach falls out of my body. "What?"

"It's not a big deal." She shrugs. "Just wasn't in my family's budget this year."

I furrow my brow. Theater camp is pretty expensive. I'm aware of that. My parents put away money for it all throughout the year so they don't have to come up with a big chunk all at once. But Cara's family doesn't have money problems. Her dad's a manager at a company that sells vacation packages to tourists and her mom is an actuary. Cara has never once mentioned financial difficulties before.

But if she's lying about finances being the issue, then . . . why isn't she going? And why didn't she say something before now?

"How come you didn't tell us?" I ask.

"I don't know. They asked me a while ago how bad I wanted to go, and then I kind of forgot about it."

Sam and I share a glance. Cara doesn't forget anything. And it sounds to me like it's only not in her family's budget because she didn't make them think she wanted to go. Did she . . . not want to go?

"Well, that's a bummer," Sam says. "It won't be as fun without you."

"Oh, stop. You don't even see me that much while we're there. You two will be fine." Cara smiles. It's sterile.

Samantha and I both go to theater camp for the acting, and Cara goes for production. It's true that a lot of the time we're apart, but everyone comes together for the big play we put on at the end of the week. Plus, there's meals and free time and all that.

"It'll be weird," I say, but I leave it at that.

"You can hang out with me that week," says Margaret, saving us all from the web of awkwardness.

"Sure," Cara says, with that same empty smile as before.

I don't know what her problem is today. Lately. All summer. She's been so hard to pin down. I can't get her to do anything if we haven't planned it in advance. I'm afraid she needs something more out of our friendship, only I can't figure out what.

"What a nice day." Sam relaxes against her pool float, eyes closed. "Pretty sure I'm gonna regret not wearing sunscreen, though."

"Told you," says Margaret dryly.

"Yeah, yeah. You're always right." Samantha opens one eye and peeks over at Margaret with a fond smile. Margaret laughs and squeezes her hand.

"Remember when my brother convinced us that we should put on coconut oil instead of sunscreen?" I say to Cara.

"Ouch!" Margaret hugs herself with her arms.

"Yeah." Cara's smile is a little warmer now. "We looked like lobsters. Mailee's mom was *so* mad."

"It was worth it." I smile devilishly at the memory. "The sunburn only hurt for a couple days but he was in a *lot* of trouble."

My brother, Hugh, is two and a half years older than me, and when we were young, he took full advantage of how gullible I was. I thought he was so wise when he went to middle school, I would believe anything he said.

"Hey, looks like your boy is summoning us." Samantha points.

Gavin's standing at the edge of the deck, beckoning us with big waves of both arms.

"What a dork," I say fondly, and start to reel us back to shore with our rope.

It is not graceful. Mainly because Sam keeps trying to help by paddling her arms, except all she's doing is turning us in circles. We're all laughing—and soaked—by the time we get back to shore.

As soon as we climb onto the deck, I hug Gavin with my dripping, ice-cold limbs. He flinches instinctively.

"Evil," he says, then kisses me.

We all take our cheeseburgers and paper plates and sit on whatever surfaces we can find. I'm in a camp chair and Gavin sits at my feet, his back against my shins. It's quite a display of trust, considering that I'm eating my food just above his head. Jackson and Cara sit beside us, but they're not talking to each other. Or touching, or anything. Actually, have I seen them speak to each other at all since we got here? I don't think I have. Hopefully, nothing bad's going on there.

Cara takes a tiny bite out of her burger, chews it slowly, and sets it down.

"Is it too rare?" Jackson asks. There, now they're talking, at least. "I tried to make sure none of them were. I know you don't like that."

"It's fine. Just not hungry." She picks at the bun, but doesn't really eat any of that, either.

When we're finished, Jackson takes all our trash to the bins they keep at the front of the house and I say I'm going to the bathroom—but I follow him instead.

"Hey." I lean against the doorway, startling him as he closes the trash bin. "Has Cara seemed a little . . . different to you lately?"

"Yeah," he says with a frown. "She's being a real—"

"Remember," I interrupt sharply, "that she is my best friend, so choose your words wisely."

"Sorry. Yeah. She's been . . . unhappy, it seems like. I don't know what I'm doing wrong."

He frowns, brow furrowed like he's concentrating on not getting upset. I fold my arms to resist the urge to hug him or something. Jackson and I get along, but we're definitely not at hugging level.

It's just, I understand exactly how he feels.

And I don't know how to fix it, either.

FOUR

I have been pacing the entryway of our house since the moment I received a text from my brother saying his flight landed. He goes to college in Denver, and he's spending the summer there, interning at a wildlife refuge. Like we don't have enough of those in Montana, but whatever. Today, he's coming home for a long weekend, and I am so excited.

It's funny; when I was a freshman and he was a senior, I couldn't wait for him to graduate and get out of the house. Now that he's been away, I actually miss him a lot.

I get another text. It's just Mom: Make sure Hugh sees that Dad baked cookies!!!!!

Hugh decided to come home pretty last minute, so neither of our parents could get the day off work. Mom is dying about it. She wanted to call in sick, but she had too many meetings. Hugh and I aren't very similar in most ways, but our inability to plan ahead, that's something we share.

A car I don't recognize pulls into the driveway and it turns out to be Hugh's rental. I run out to greet him. He hugs me and then says, "I'm assuming you came out to carry in all my stuff for me."

"Please. Yeah, right."

He laughs, shouldering a duffel bag and handing me his battered laptop. "I'm a guest, you have to carry *something*."

"You so do not count as a guest. Dad made cookies, by the way."

I take his laptop, and when he sets down his duffel bag right inside the doorway, I drop the computer on top of it.

He grabs a cookie from the kitchen and holds out another one to me.

"I don't know," I say. "Mom and Dad made it *very clear* that these cookies are for you, not me."

He grins. "I won't tell."

I take the cookie. Truth is, I've already eaten two. "How was your flight?"

"Short. Which is the best kind of flight, I guess."

My phone dings with another text message. This one's from Cara, and it just says, maybe.

I sigh. I texted her this morning to tell her Hugh was coming and she should stop by sometime this weekend to see him. A maybe from her means no, lately. And it's pretty much the only answer she's been giving me, too. Last time I saw her was at the lake five days ago.

"Hey, Hugh?" I break a piece off my cookie, rocking anxiously back on my heels. "When you were a senior in high school, did any of your friends . . . did things get weird?"

Hugh's an odd choice to talk about this with. I mean, he's a boy, first of all. And he's never had a friendship like mine and Cara's. He had a group, the kind where there didn't seem to be one person he felt more strongly about than the others. But, I don't know, sometimes he has good advice.

"Everything gets a little weird when you're a senior," he says, shoving a big bite of cookie into his mouth. "Which of your friends is the problem?"

"Cara."

"Huh. Well, summers are hard for her now, aren't they?"

"Yeah. I guess." Maybe he's right. Last summer was definitely rough; it was the first full summer since the car accident, and Harper's absence was gaping. Cara had been watching Harper during school breaks since she was twelve, which meant, pretty much, so had I. And then last year, whenever we went swimming, I'd have this moment of panic where I'd scan the beach for Harper, forgetting that she wasn't there. Forgetting that I hadn't lost her because she was already gone. Or Cara would pick me up to go to the mall, and I'd half turn to say hi to Harper in the backseat before remembering it was empty. However keenly I felt that loss, Cara felt it tenfold. But she was still Cara. She organized things, she planned things, she helped me clean my room.

This summer, she feels like . . . a shell.

"You've been friends a long time," Hugh says. "*Too* long. Whatever's going on with you two, she'll get over it."

"I hope so. Thanks." I slide into a kitchen chair. "So, you need to tell me all about your internship. Mom explained it to me but I'm not totally sure she even understands what you're doing."

Hugh grabs four more cookies and launches into a long explanation. He's clearly loving the job, traipsing around in the forest all day. He's always been the only woodsy one in our family. My parents had to send him to outdoorsy camps and endure 4-H programs and Boy Scouts because neither of them knows anything about that stuff.

It strikes me that suddenly everyone in my life seems to be into nature—Hugh, Gavin, now Cara with the Haven, which she's brought up multiple times since our visit. I'm pretty sure they're all insane. *In*side is where you don't get rained on or eaten by a bear.

Or trapped in a root cellar. *Shiver*.

"Are you going to have Gavin come over?" Hugh asks. "It'd be cool to see him."

His tone is nonchalant, but my brother is surprisingly into my boyfriend. Gavin knows about a lot of stuff that Hugh is interested in. They've only met once, and Hugh spent about three hours grilling Gavin about cows and hunting and trapping. It was totally boring, but also gave me a strong sensation of pride in my chest. My boyfriend is so great that my college-aged brother thinks he's cool.

"I'll see what he's up to," I say, and send Gavin a text. He replies quickly. "He said he's doing some chores with his dad right now, but he'll come over in a bit."

Hugh shrugs like he didn't care one way or the other, but I know he's hoping it'll be soon.

An hour or so later, when Hugh and I are watching reruns on TV, I get another text from Cara. I'm coming over, it says.

That's . . . surprising.

"Guess Cara's coming over after all," I say.

"Cool." Hugh has moved from cookies to chips. He is really making the most of this weekend, already, eating his way through all the junk foods in our house. "Is she still dating that guy or should I look presentable?"

I glare at him. "Yes she is, and ew."

He's joking, mostly. But in the past couple years, as Cara and I have gotten older, he's started to make jokes more often about dating her, and I don't even know what I would do if he tried. Die, probably. She's pretty, and it's fine if he wants to notice that, but he needs to notice it from afar.

Less than five minutes later, Cara explodes into my house, a whirlwind of chaos. Her face is blotchy, eyes bloodshot.

"What happened? Are you okay?" I leap up from the couch in alarm, hurrying to her side.

"Jackson and I had a big fight," she says. "I just broke up with him."

Before I've worked out what to say, Jackson bursts in the door behind her. This is a nightmare.

"Um, heard of knocking?" I snap at him. I don't know what happened yet, but I know I'm Team Cara.

He ignores me altogether. "You can't break up with me and then just *leave*," he shouts, much too close to Cara's face. "I don't even know what I did!"

"I obviously didn't want to talk about it anymore." She wipes fiercely at tears streaming down her face. "That's why I came here. You know what you did. I *told* you what you did."

"You've gone totally crazy." He scowls at her.

I hover nearby, anxious. I want to intervene. Seeing Cara weeping infuriates me, sets me on fire with the need to eliminate the source of her pain. But it's not my fight, and I don't want to make it worse.

"We're always fighting lately," she shouts at Jackson through her tears. "We both know that we're not going to stay together once we leave for college, so we might as well not spend the next year miserable and yelling at each other."

"That is so—" Jackson sucks in an angry breath. "I can't believe you would do this. I wasted more than a year on you. And what was even the point? So you could break up with me over one dumb fight? Good luck finding someone else who will put up with your crap for as long as I did without you even putting out."

"*Whoa.*" I step between them, sparkling with rage. "Not cool, Jackson. You need to leave. Now."

"I'm not done—"

"Now," Hugh says quietly, slipping between us.

Jackson hesitates a moment longer, but Hugh is big enough to be intimidating. Combined with the quiet assertiveness, especially.

I close my eyes against the sound of Jackson slamming our front door.

Cara slumps against the wall, looking vulnerable and defeated. I feel . . . the opposite. Relieved that she came to me, that she needs me after all. Maybe it makes me monstrous, but I've been so worried.

Now I'm getting my chance to fix things.

FIVE

I drive a sobbing Cara back to her house in Hugh's car, while he promises to explain to Gavin what happened, if Gavin shows up at mine. This whole thing is a mess I am totally unprepared to deal with. I want to help, but I don't know how.

So I pull out the best weapon in my arsenal: ice cream. We sit in Cara's kitchen, eating directly from a carton. *I* probably don't need the ice cream, but you know. Solidarity. Any excuse to eat some. Cara's barely nibbling at it.

"So what happened this morning?" I ask.

"I don't know." She drops her face into her hands. "We were fighting, and lately it feels like we're *always* fighting. I just . . . didn't want to be together anymore. And I didn't want to talk about it, either. I just wanted it to be over. Have you ever felt like that? Like you were just . . . *done*? We were in his car, and I knew your house was a lot closer than mine, so I got out and fled, basically. But, of course, he followed me."

I lean across the kitchen island and squeeze her arm. "I'm so sorry. I don't even know what to say. I didn't realize you guys were having such a hard time." Even if I sort of did.

She lifts her face from her hands. "Was I wrong? Should I not have broken up with him?"

I hesitate, not because I think she *is* wrong, but because I'm worried about why she did it. About why they've been fighting more. About whether it even has anything to do with Jackson himself. "If you weren't happy, then staying together doesn't benefit either of you. I mean, what is it you argue about?"

"Oh, everything. Today it was him pressuring me about sex. Same old."

That settles a sour feeling deep in my gut. "You didn't owe him your virginity just because you'd been together for a year. You know that."

She grimaces.

"Cara. Tell me you know that."

"I know that. I do." She jabs her spoon into the ice cream, which she's still barely touched. "I just feel so mixed up. I was in love with him. If you love someone, aren't you supposed to want to stay with them?"

I don't know what to say. Cara's not an impulsive person. If she did this, some part of her has been thinking it through for a while.

"Maybe I never loved him at all," she goes on. "Maybe I only thought I did. I don't know anything, Mailee. I just don't know anything anymore."

"You know more than you think. Look how he acted at my house. It's not okay to shame you for being a virgin, especially not in front of your friends. He doesn't get to decide when you're ready. And pressuring you like that wasn't helpful. I know it's going to hurt for a while, but I think you're so much better off."

"Thanks, Mailee. I'm sorry for ruining your day. Your brother's home and everything, you don't have to be here with me."

"Stop. You didn't ruin anything. You run my whole life for me. I think the least I can do is reciprocate by eating ice cream with you when you're going through a breakup."

She lets out a tiny laugh, and I feel my shoulders finally relax. "I hope the burden of eating ice cream isn't too much for you to bear."

"It is a heavy one, but I'll try to get through it."

She sighs deeply. "This really sucks. I feel so . . . I wanted it to end better. But I guess . . . well, Firehorse said that the greatest decisions of our lives are preceded by chaos, so maybe this is my chaos."

"Firehorse? Like, the guy who lives in the woods?"

"Yeah."

"When did he say that?"

She opens her mouth to answer me, but just then we hear her mom getting home. Cara wipes quickly at her eyes, but it doesn't hide anything.

"Hi, Mrs. Pearlman," I say politely.

"Hi, Mailee. Cara, what's wrong?"

"Relationship stuff, Mom. No offense, but I don't really want to talk about it."

Cara's mom has her same honey-blonde hair. It's been going gray pretty rapidly over the past couple years, but you don't notice unless you're standing close to her.

"Okay," she says hesitantly. "If you really don't want to."

She doesn't stick around. Her footsteps echo from the stairs leading up to the bedrooms. Cara and her mom used to talk about everything. In fact, Cara's mom coached us both through using a tampon for the first time. She was full of life and fire. She used to read lines with me sometimes, and she'd get really into it.

I hadn't realized until this moment how much I missed that.

"Is everything else okay?" I ask hesitantly.

"Of course," Cara says breezily. A standard, easy response. And nothing more.

"You can always talk to me, you know. You don't have to take this stuff all on yourself."

She smiles faintly.

"It's just things with Jackson. Everything will be fine now," she says, like she's convincing herself. "Everything will be great."

I nod. Of course she's right.

She always is.

SIX

I'm simultaneously exhausted and amped up when I get home. Mom's car is parked out front—I *knew* she would find a way to leave work early—and I open the front door to the sound of her laughter. She sits together with Hugh and Gavin in the living room, which is more than a little terrifying. Not only is this the first time Gavin's been alone with my brother, but we're adding my mom? God only knows what kind of embarrassing stories she saw fit to tell him about me.

Gavin, sitting in the armchair, notices me first. "How's Cara doing?"

"About like you'd expect." I frown. "But she'll be okay."

Mom turns to glance at me from where she sits beside Hugh on the couch. "I heard it was an eventful morning!"

"It was." I sigh. "But I was more of a bystander than a participant."

I want to talk to Gavin—alone—but I don't know how to accomplish that with Mom sitting right there. She trusts me with him, but usually when he comes up to my room, my parents are still at work. Or I'm already in there so he just passes through the house.

Hugh saves me. "Hey, Mom, I have some pictures from my internship on my laptop; want to see?"

When they leave, I'm able to usher Gavin upstairs with minimum awkwardness.

"So what happened, exactly?" he asks when I've closed the door behind us. "Your brother filled me in a little, but . . ."

I sum up the morning's drama as best I can, stumbling a bit when I get to the part where Jackson was a royal jerk about Cara's virginity.

Gavin and I haven't slept together, either. Gavin seems to respect that I'm not ready, but Jackson had told Cara he was okay with it, too. What if, by the time we've been together a year, I'm still not ready and Gavin's not okay with it? I try to suppress the little voice of worry in the back of my mind, the voice that's been chewing on my brain since I heard Jackson's words. He and Gavin aren't the same person. But when something like this happens to your beautiful best friend, it's hard to believe it won't happen to you, too.

"What is it?" Gavin says, and by the caution in his tone, it's clear that he knows exactly what I'm thinking about.

"You would tell me, right?" I say. "If you were unhappy about the pace things are going? You wouldn't, like, save it to throw in my face during fights? I'm not saying it'll be a year before I'm ready, but I'm not saying it *won't* be, either."

"Mailee." He presses a hand gently to my cheek, but there's hurt in his eyes. I regret saying anything. "I just want to be with you. The rest will come when it comes."

"That's what my head is telling me," I say, holding on to a fistful of his shirt. "But my heart is being a little insecure."

"Tell your heart to shut up, then."

I laugh. "I'll try, but it's notorious for ignoring my commands."

He hugs me tight and I realize that what I'm feeling isn't actually insecurity at all; it's guilt. Gavin is the perfect boyfriend. He is sweet and understanding and he never tries to make me feel bad about anything. I wouldn't be so dramatic as to say I don't *deserve* him, because I think unless you're a horrible monster of a human being, deciding who you do or don't deserve is pretty unfair to yourself. But what I *do* feel is that there is no way on this earth I deserve to have a sweet, wonderful, perfect boyfriend more than Cara does. Her life has been so much harder than mine. And yet, she's a big part of why mine's so easy.

Maybe I shouldn't blame Jackson for whatever went wrong between the two of them. Maybe he's the perfect boyfriend, for someone else. But I can't help the bitter ache in my chest when I think about the way he talked to her, or about how she must have felt when he pressured her about sex.

Gavin presses his lips to my forehead. His fingers trail along my jaw, tilting my face up until I meet his gaze. It's hard to be upset when he's looking at me like I'm the world. When his fingertips are tickling my skin, and I'm starting to feel feverish and ignited. He kisses me in gentle brushes of his mouth on mine. I run my hands up under his shirt, because I like how the smooth skin of his abs feels against my fingers. He sighs and kisses me harder, weaving his hands into my hair.

"Is it bad that when Jackson was mean to Cara, I wanted to rip the skin off his face?" I murmur.

Gavin bursts out laughing. "I mean, it's a little bit *Silence of the Lambs . . .*"

"I should have done it."

"I did *not* know you had this sadistic side to you. Should I be worried?"

"Probably not." But I frown, because his use of the word *worried* reminds me of something else I wanted to mention. "Hey, there was this thing Cara said after I brought her home that was a little . . . uh. She said Firehorse told her something like 'our greatest decisions are preceded by chaos,' and the way she said it made me wonder if she's seen or talked to him since we all went to the commune that day. She mentions that place a lot, but usually it's just about how sweet Avalon was. This felt like . . . more. I don't know. Maybe I'm reading too much into it."

"Hmm." Gavin furrows his brow. "Did you ask her if she had gone back?"

"I asked her when he said it, but her mom interrupted and she never ended up answering me. Do you think I should tell her that thing about the girl who died in the freezer? I mean, if she's still going there . . ."

"I'd find out if she's still in contact with the Haven first. But yeah. I think you should tell her about that. Just so she knows and doesn't end up blindsided, if nothing else."

After we came back from visiting the commune, I told Gavin as soon as I possibly could about going into the root cellar with Alexa. We both agreed that while it's a creepy story that makes neither of us ever want to go into a walk-in freezer, it seems like she was telling the truth. That it was an unfortunate accident and everything. I just needed a second opinion, really, to make sure I wasn't being crazy for not calling the police.

I honestly haven't thought about it much since. But if Cara's still interested in that place, still talking to those people . . . it only seems right that she should know someone died there.

I lean into Gavin's chest, inhale his boyish scent.

"At least one good thing's come out of this," he says, wrapping his arms around me.

"Yeah? What's that?"

"You can add 'wanting to rip the skin off someone's face' to your emotions journal."

"True," I say, laughing. "That's definitely a new one."

SEVEN

The next week, Cara convinces me to go with her to the Haven again. She used her signature pout (seriously, no one can pout like Cara—I've tried to emulate it so many times for acting purposes and it's impossible), and the fact that she just went through a breakup as leverage. I tried to get out of it by telling her the root cellar story, but she already knew it.

"Alexa told me when I went the other day," she said, but she wasn't clear on when "the other day" was, or why she went a second time without telling me. "She thought you got freaked out by the story and she felt bad."

"I didn't get freaked out by it," I muttered, even though it was a lie. "But I'm surprised it didn't bother you."

She shrugged. "I understand their pain, I guess."

That ended any further discussion on that, and I had no choice but to agree to come.

I wasn't going to bring Gavin anyway, but Cara tells me he's not exactly welcome, even if I wanted to. I do text him that we're going, though, and he replies with: Drive carefully and don't become a vegan ;)

Cute.

Or at least, I thought so. Cara was less amused when I showed it to her.

It's a hot day, and when we arrive at the Haven, we discover that everyone is swimming. Or, most everyone, anyway. Fire-horse isn't here. He's been gone the past couple days, the others tell us. And this is no big deal, apparently. He just goes from time to time, off into the woods somewhere. It actually makes me respect him more. If you're going to lead a commune that's all about living in nature, I feel like you should be capable of surviving on your own in nature.

Plus, the environment's more relaxed without him around, I notice. Maybe it's just me. The pressure to impress these people is lower without him, somehow. Everyone else intimidates me less.

Avalon runs up to Cara the second we're out of the car, wrapping her arms around Cara's thighs. "I'm so glad you're here!" she exclaims. Cara lights up like a Christmas tree.

We didn't bring bathing suits, so we borrow from girls who live here. I'm not super modest, and usually I feel fine in a bathing suit. But I also spend a lot of time picking one out each year, making sure it's flattering. I'd never admit it to anyone, but I still haven't quite lost the anxiety that always accompanied beach trips when I was in middle school—when I was all ribs and elbows and knobby knees, before my body started to have some kind of shape to it, before I learned how to let insults about my slight build roll off me. But the bathing suit I'm wearing right now . . . it's not flattering at all. It brings me back to those days where I felt exposed and weird-shaped. And the bottom piece is slightly too big, which means part of me is concentrating on making sure it doesn't slip down my nonexistent butt.

"Come on, Mailee!" one of the girls shouts to me. It's Alexa. Cara's already in the water, splashing around with Avalon. Watching them, I wonder how it feels to be the only kid in a place like this. Maybe she doesn't know anything different; maybe she feels spoiled by all the adults doting on her.

I get brave, and leap from the end of the dock, cannon-balling into the water and raining a gigantic wave over anyone who didn't get out of my way quick enough. When I surface, Cara is laughing in front of me, her face dripping with water.

"You are such a jerk," she says.

"That insult would hold a lot more weight if you weren't laughing yourself to death while you said it."

She splashes me, and I splash her back. Soon we're in a full-on war. What's left of my mascara is probably all over my face, but I don't care. The water's nice, refreshing. With my toes touching the bottom, I'm chest deep, which eases my bathing suit anxiety.

Avalon joins us. She's a good swimmer for a kid her age. Alexa doesn't even seem worried about her. She's off near the dock, talking to a couple other girls, and hasn't even glanced our way.

Cara doesn't seem to mind, though. She twirls Avalon in the water and they laugh together like they've known each other their whole lives. This is the most relaxed I've seen Cara in . . . I can't even remember how long.

"Do you want to see the frog eggs I found?" Avalon asks.

"Definitely!"

Cara doesn't spare me a second glance before she wades back toward shore with Avalon, and disappears behind a patch of cattails.

I take the opportunity to glance around. You'd think that with about two dozen residents all swimming here, it'd feel really crowded, but it doesn't. Not everyone is staying near the dock, though. Some swim farther out, some are off to the side, fishing.

. . . *Fishing?*

"Hey, aren't you guys vegan?" I ask a girl who's near me, pointing.

She glances toward the small group casting lines into the water. "Oh, yeah. Sometimes people like to fish. They throw them back."

"Oh. Good."

Here's the thing. I've been fishing. I mean, only, like, three times because worms are gritty and fish are slimy. But I know that you can have the best intentions and still potentially kill a fish by accident. Those hooks are sharp and sometimes the fish swallow them. I feel like if you are a commune of people who are vegan for animal rights reasons . . . I don't know. Shouldn't that bother you?

I'm overthinking. Cara would tell me I'm overthinking if she weren't so busy perusing the shoreline with Avalon.

"I'm Brigit, by the way," says the girl I just spoke to.

"I'm Mailee."

She laughs. "Of course I know who *you* are. It's not every day we get visitors."

"Do you like living here?" I ask, which is a totally dumb question, but I've only really talked to Alexa and Firehorse so far, and I'm curious how other people feel. Brigit is black, and she's the only person I've seen here who isn't white. It's not entirely surprising—Montana is a pretty white place—but I wonder if it's uncomfortable being the only one who isn't.

"It's better here than anywhere else I've ever lived." She waves a hand to drive off a flying insect that dives at her face. "I've just . . . never quite *belonged* anywhere. And here, I do. I felt welcome from day one."

"People here are definitely nice," I agree. My eyes sweep back to the group that's fishing. "Except that one guy seems kinda glowery."

Brigit giggles. "Yeah, Finn? He's actually a good guy. Just not too trusting of strangers. He's been with Firehorse since the beginning, basically. I think he was the first member recruited to the commune. So he's a little protective. We've got a good vibe here, and a wrong person can totally sour it, you know?"

"Yeah, that makes sense." Am *I* a wrong person? Finn didn't glare at Cara the way he glares at me. I feel like a virus, poised to sweep through and destroy the whole group without warning.

There's also something to the way she said it, something bitter. It makes me think of Opal, the girl who died. And of the way Alexa seemed to blame Opal for what happened to her. It seems like maybe there's a bit of a survival-of-the-fittest mentality here.

"Do you ever get to see your families?" I ask, and then hope it's not too personal of a question.

"If anyone desperately wanted to, sure, but we're here to get away from all that stuff, you know? A lot of people here have bad families to begin with. And outside people tend to bring in toxic stuff, too, which isn't necessarily good for us."

"Toxic stuff?"

Brigit furrows her brow. "You really weren't told much about us, huh? Didn't Firehorse give you a link to his site? Usually he gives it to everyone."

"I, uh . . . he gave me the link. I've just been kinda busy." Pretty much the weakest excuse I could've come up with, but she lets it pass.

"It's worth a read," she says. "I know you're not here to move in, but it's still good stuff to think about. You feel so much better, healthier out here, away from all the poisons in the air and in the food, but even back in civilization there's things you can do to protect yourself."

"I'll read the site," I promise. And I really might. Who knows. "How long have you lived here?"

"A couple years. Everyone here has been with us at least a year now. We haven't been recruiting lately," says Brigit. "Firehorse keeps saying that we don't need anyone else, unless someone really good comes along, someone really necessary."

Necessary. Huh.

"How do you know if someone's necessary?"

She shrugs. "That's above my pay grade."

"You get paid to live here?"

She laughs. "No, no. That's just a joking way of telling you it's not a group decision."

"Oh." My cheeks flame with embarrassment because, yeah, I'm a moron. "I guess I didn't realize you actually recruited members. I figured you all just kinda found each other."

"I mean, it's not like the military." She shrugs. "And a lot of people ended up here because of Firehorse's website, but it's easier to keep a place like this running if you have the right numbers. There's a balance between making sure you don't have so many mouths to feed that it becomes unsustainable, but having enough hands to get all our tasks done. Cara must have told you about how scheduled we are?"

She told me no such thing, but I nod anyway.

"Yeah, she seemed to really like that aspect. Anyway, it's hard to get all the things done in a day that need to be done if there aren't enough people to do it."

"Well, it's nice that you guys have let Cara and me visit, even though we probably disrupt your schedule," I say. "We're obviously not gonna be moving in."

"No?" Her eyes dart to Cara, who's still hanging out with Avalon and a couple other girls. She's totally relaxed, happy. But why wouldn't she be? Everyone's just hanging out. It's no different from being at the beach anywhere else.

I laugh it off, though. "Of course not. We're starting our senior year this fall. And then we're going to college in LA, hopefully. Or New York, if not."

Brigit's mouth twists. "I hope all of that works out for you, Mailee," she says earnestly. "Commune life isn't for everyone, and it sounds like you know what you want, so . . . I hope it all goes like you dreamed."

"Thank you."

My stomach twists into a knot. The way Brigit says it is like she doubts things *will* work out like I planned, and that's ridiculous. It's immortalized in the Book of Life Goals. And so far, everything Cara and I have added to our plan in that thing has worked out perfectly. Maybe there've been a few bumps in the road this summer, but we're still on track.

I'm starting to get chilly, so I excuse myself and wade back to the dock. I can lounge in the sun for a little while, maybe.

As I reach for the wooden ladder to pull myself out onto the rough wooden planks, something big and brownish black with too many legs scurries across *right* where I was about to touch. I yank back my hand and let out a bloodcurdling shriek, and much to my embarrassment, everyone stops talking so they can turn and stare at me.

"Dock spider," I say in a shaking voice.

It is so gross. My skin crawls. I don't want to be anywhere near it. With its gigantic body and its inches-long legs and the way it just appeared out of nowhere. Like a giant baby, I stand in front of the dock and wait until someone comes and shoos the spider away.

"It's okay," Alexa says, herding it off the ladder with a brush of her fingertips. I want to throw up. "I was afraid of them at first, too."

"And then what?" I ask in a voice that was meant to be light and joking but is still wobbling. "Did someone throw a bucket of them over you so you got acclimated?"

Thankfully, she laughs. "We do a lot of camping. Spiders aren't so bad once you've seen enough of them."

I have seen *plenty* of spiders in my day and I would have to disagree. But I guess if I lived in a metal shack in the woods, maybe I'd feel differently.

Except no. I wouldn't.

Alexa follows me as I make my hurried escape from the dock. "I have towels in my house," she says. "You can get dried off there."

I guess technically these shacks *are* their houses, but it's jarring to hear her call it that. They're so small, so unhouselike. And I hadn't planned to get dried off yet—I was just going to come sit on the beach. But she's already walking away without me, so I throw a nervous glance behind me and then follow her. Cara seems fine hanging out with the others in the water, so I don't know what I'm worried about.

When we reach the shack, I notice that there's the same logo carved into it as there was in the door to the root cellar. It's not hard to guess what the *H* stands for—Haven. But I'm curious about the Latin word *verum*, and its relevance to this place. The shack's metal door opens with a shriek. Inside, it's pretty dark. Sunlight can't pierce the metal, and there's only one small, high window. It's stuffy, though. The metal's heated up from the outside, and allows little air flow. The floorboards are wood, and two camping cots with blow-up mattresses take up nearly two entire walls. An overstuffed bin of toys sits near the door, with a dresser along another wall. A couple high shelves hold books, and a super-tiny end table perched next to one of the beds holds a gas lamp. And that's pretty much it. I know tiny living is, like, a trend right now, but whoa.

"Hey, so what is it that made you decide to come back?" Alexa asks me the second her door closes.

"Cara wanted to," I say. "It seemed to mean a lot to her."

"But what about *you*?" Alexa asks. She's being really intense and she's super close to me, majorly piercing my personal bubble.

"I don't know." I take the towel she offers. "That's really all. I didn't want to say no to Cara. She's having a pretty rough time right now."

"That's nice," Alexa says, backing off a little. "I'm glad that you're such a good friend to her. But this place, it's not a joke or something to come and gawk at, you know? We live here. It matters to us. This is our home and our life and if you're not serious about it, you shouldn't be here."

"I know that." I feel a tad guilty because I *did* come the first time with a little bit of an observing-creatures-in-their-habitat mentality and that's definitely not fair. But it isn't why I'm here now. "I didn't mean to make you feel disrespected by coming back here. Cara seems pretty attached to your daughter. She lost a sister who was right at that age, and it only happened a couple years ago."

Alexa frowns thoughtfully. "I didn't know that. I'm so sorry."

"Hadn't you noticed how quickly she got attached to Avalon?"

Alexa shrugs. "I figured she was one of those people who really loves kids. You know the type. She's been *great* with Avalon, though. If she were here all the time . . . it'd be wonderful."

"She won't be, though." My voice is harsher than I meant. I'm starting to get a little worked up at everyone for trying to keep Cara.

"I know, I know."

Alexa smiles placatingly, but I'm worried that I'm coming off like a jerk again.

"Anyway, I promise, I have nothing but respect for you. I couldn't live like this." I gesture to the living quarters before me. "I think it's really cool that you live off the land. And that you're not afraid of spiders."

She smiles. "I used to miss it all. The city, the electricity. All the shopping and TV shows and everything else you all do outside of here. For the first year I lived here, whenever I'd go into town, I'd get jealous. I wondered if I'd made a mistake, and I thought maybe I should try to find a job and an apartment and move back. But there's more to it than just the amenities. There's so much more. I'd never try to explain it all to you because Firehorse does it so much better, but, Mailee . . ." She pauses to reach for my hand. The hair raises on the back of my neck. "Just think about all the things you believe. Question them. Really dig into them. Things are very wrong in this world. *Very* wrong. A place like this . . . we might just be a little safer from it all."

She lets go of my hand, slowly, fingers sliding against my palm as she releases me. I suppress a shiver. It feels like she's relaying some sort of message to me, but I don't know what it is. I'm not naïve. I know the world is not a sunshine and rainbow place, but her tone almost makes things seem . . . dire. Like it's all going to come crashing down.

If it does all come crashing down, though, is this where I'd want to be? I don't think so. What difference would it make? Let's get apocalyptic here, and picture some kind of nuclear explosion gone wrong, or a meteor, or some other cataclysmic event. Is being out here going to help me survive any longer? Maybe, but how much longer? And would I even want to, knowing I was just prolonging the inevitable, and doing it away from my family and my boyfriend and my friends?

And if the world goes to war . . . that's a much realer concern, but I doubt Montana is target number one, and I doubt it matters if I'm nestled in the woods or if I'm in town.

"Is that . . . what the purpose is, of this place? To, like, be sheltered from . . . from, you know, everything?" That did *not* come out well and I probably offended her again, but oh well.

"I mean, there's not a *purpose*, exactly. Firehorse wanted to be away from all the technology and the propaganda and the lies, so he bought this land about five years ago, and came up here to live with a few of the others. Being out here, it clears us of all the toxins in the modern world, all the electromagnetic waves and the mercury poisoning and the filth—everything. We usually get a new addition or two every year, though Firehorse has been getting pickier. There can only be so many of us, you know? Otherwise the resources of the land get stretched too thin."

It's hard for me to imagine the resources around here getting stretched too thin, but combining this with what Brigit said earlier, it makes sense.

"Do you ever miss your family?"

Her face darkens, and I regret my question immediately.

"I'm sorry. I shouldn't have asked you that. It was too personal." Me and my mouth, seriously.

"No, no, it's okay." She waves a hand. "I do miss them, sometimes. But I missed them before I came here, too. Before I stopped living with them. My parents were so embarrassed that their daughter had a baby at seventeen. They could barely look at me. I knew they didn't want me living with them anymore, but they didn't know what to do with me. I graduated high school, but I couldn't even think about college. I was overwhelmed at the thought of going out of state, by myself, with Avalon. But to stay and just, like, bear their judgment every day? I couldn't deal with that, either. Meeting Firehorse felt like stars aligning. It saved me from all of that. So yeah, I miss them sometimes. And I wonder if they miss me. But they were done with me long before I came here. I told them I was leaving and they didn't care one bit."

"Wow. That's . . . I can't imagine my parents doing that to me."

Her mouth twists into a sad smile. "Neither could I."

She pushes open the door of her house with another shriek of metal, and we step back out into the sunlight. I feel like I'm looking at everything about this place with new eyes, after talking to her. It's not just a commune where everyone eats vegetables and works the land. It's a saving grace for people who felt unwanted, abandoned. There's a little ache of fondness in my heart now, for Firehorse. He might be weird, but look at the good he's doing here.

"Alexa!"

We both jump at the sound of a sharp male voice calling her name. It's Firehorse, who is at the bottom of a steep path leading up into the trees. He strides toward us, face set in displeasure, and the fondness I was starting to feel subsides.

"Cara's here, too," says Alexa without so much as a greeting. "And Mailee and I just had a great talk."

A long look passes between them. I can't read it, but I don't like it. When Cara asked to come back here, it had never once occurred to me that I wasn't welcome, but more and more I'm feeling like these people just are not at all fans of me. It makes me self-conscious. I like to think I'm a pretty nice girl. But maybe not everyone feels that way? No one at school seems to hate me. I'm too deep into drama club to be mainstream popular, but no one ever acts like my mere presence offends them the way these two are doing right now.

"It's nice to see you again," I say, holding out my hand to Firehorse.

"Yes." He gives me one of his big smiles. "It's nice to see you again, too."

"I'll gather everyone," Alexa says. "Now that you're back."

"Thank you." He squeezes her forearm and she stares up at him for a long moment. I look away because it's kind of intimate and I wonder if something is going on there. They're both adults, so I guess that's okay, but Firehorse is still a *lot* older than Alexa. "And please let them know I'm disappointed."

She scurries off and I'm alone with Firehorse, which is just great. I look at his cheaply made dreamcatcher necklace and for Gavin's sake, I want to ask what store he bought it from. So he feels embarrassed.

But I don't quite have the spine to mention it.

"So, Mailee," Firehorse says politely. "What compelled you to return to our little corner of the woods?"

"Cara," I say simply.

"Ah, I see."

The others are returning from the water now. There's a weird vibe coming off them. They don't seem sad, exactly, but the carefree laughter is gone. They're very quiet.

Were they expecting Firehorse to be gone longer? What was he disappointed about? Were they not supposed to be swimming?

"Hey, Mailee." Brigit grabs my arm. "Want to help us prepare lunch?"

"Definitely."

I'm relieved to be away from Firehorse, who I'm pretty sure is simmering under the surface with some serious irritation. Brigit gives me some carrots to slice, and she doesn't say much after that. Everyone else is doing chores, too. I spot Cara with some of the others putting away firewood. I don't want to be difficult again, but I have all these questions and I feel like if I don't ask, they're going to clog up my lungs.

"Were you guys, um, not supposed to be swimming?" I ask timidly.

Brigit barely glances at me. She's sprinkling garlic between slices of a loaf of bread. Garlic bread without butter on it? No thanks.

"We have a schedule," Brigit says, just when I think she's going to completely ignore me. "Free time isn't till later this afternoon. But it was so nice out and we didn't think Firehorse would mind. He wasn't due back till tomorrow anyway."

"But he came back early and he caught you and he *did* mind."

Her mouth thins. "Looks that way."

I don't ask her anything else, even though I have a billion more questions. Do they get in trouble if they don't follow their schedule? Firehorse doesn't really seem to be a father figure to them, but maybe he is and I haven't seen it in my limited exposure to this place.

As I'm trying to decide whether to pry more, Firehorse comes for me. "Mailee, I would like to speak with you, please," he says.

"Where?" I ask timidly.

He gestures toward the fire pit. Plain sight. I brush off my hands, take a quick glance at Brigit—who is apparently very interested in the garlic bread at the moment—and follow him.

"Cara will always be welcome here," he says slowly, when we've sat down—too close to each other for my comfort—on one of the cut logs. I notice that he's got the circled *H* tattooed on the underside of his forearm. That's dedication. "But if you ever feel you'd like to return with her, I'm going to have to ask that you come with a different . . . aura."

Oh God.

"Um, aura?"

"Yes. You radiate a lot of skepticism. You may not be doing it verbally, but you are telling me you think I'm wrong with every movement you make. This is my home, and that's very hurtful. Did you know that Cara has visited my website? That she's working on becoming a vegan and working on having a more natural lifestyle to heal her body and mind?"

Giving up ice cream? She can't seriously be considering that. Is she? It gives me pause. If Cara is willing to give up ice cream, then does Firehorse have a legitimate point?

"I didn't know," I say meekly. "And I'm sorry if I've made you feel like I'm skeptical of everything. I'm just naturally a questioner, I guess. I mean, my boyfriend's family owns a ranch. I've been there, I've seen how they treat their animals. So I'm having a hard time with the idea that—"

"Let me stop you there," Firehorse interrupts. "Because I understand. It's hard when we are connected to someone who thinks they know a lot about the subject. But just because someone *appears* to have a lot of knowledge doesn't mean they do. Sometimes those in the farming industry are less aware than those who are outside of it."

That feels wrong, but at the same time, now I'm totally confused. What if Firehorse is right and I'm being stubborn and not giving any of it a chance?

"Just think about things, Mailee. That's all I'm asking." Firehorse pats my hand. Which sounds creepy, but he doesn't do it in a gross way. "I pride myself on my ability to relay information, you know. It's what makes me such a good leader, such a good guide for my Colonists. But I know how hard it is to get people to listen. Everyone's been so trained from such a young age to believe in certain things that they don't want to hear anything different. I would hate to see you become part of the darkness that our world is headed toward because you were too stubborn to hear other viewpoints. People often think I'm crazy for caring so much about the environment. And you don't need to pretend you haven't thought so, too. But the earth bleeds because of us, Mailee. It weeps for what humanity has done. Be part of the solution, not the problem."

I feel like I'm about one inch tall now. I've always thought I was open-minded, never thought I was the kind of person who dismissed things, unless they were the sorts of things that weren't worth listening to.

"I'm so sorry," I say. "I will definitely try to do better. I really do think that everyone here is great, and Alexa and Brigit said a lot of things to me earlier that made me realize how beneficial this place is to everyone who lives here, and how great it is that they get to have a chance to live someplace where they're not judged for things outside their control. I guess I didn't realize how close-minded I was being."

"I understand," Firehorse says with a kind smile. "And you're free to go. Thank you for speaking with me."

I get up and head awkwardly back toward the food prep area. Except more people are in there now, and I feel like maybe they don't need me. Plus, the way that Brigit was so determinedly not looking at me; I don't want to force my company on her if she's not sure she wants it. My mind is a weird haze. I'm totally unsure whether I just got manipulated by Firehorse or not. He's mad at everyone for slacking off today, but if it was that bad, would they even have dared to do it in the first place? Maybe it's like how I know my parents will take away my laptop if I act like a brat, but sometimes I do it anyway because the punishment isn't so bad that I'm terrified by it.

I spot Cara, sitting near the woodpile. She's talking to that guy Finn, the one who stared unsettlingly at me the first time we came here. There's nothing wrong with him at all. He's kind of cute, hasn't actually said or done anything to me, and Brigit said he was nice, but I get a vibe from him that I don't like. Some instinct screams *back off.* Cara doesn't seem to get that vibe, though. She's laughing at something he said, and her hand comes to rest on his forearm. He responds by squeezing her knee. Whoa.

I guess one way to get over Jackson is to flirt with someone else, like, immediately, and I can't deny her that. But I also don't want her alone with him because, like I said, the vibe. So I head over and walk into their conversation like I have no idea they were flirting three seconds ago.

"I don't think we've met," I say, holding out a hand to him. "I'm Mailee."

"I know that," he says. "Firehorse introduced you to all of us, remember? Anyway, I'm Finn."

He doesn't take my hand. Well. If he's going to be like that, then he does *not* get the privilege of flirting with my best friend.

"Cara, I think we probably ought to be heading home," I say. "We don't want to overstay our welcome."

"I don't think it's possible for Cara to overstay her welcome," says Finn.

It takes all of my skill as an actress not to roll my eyes.

"Mailee's right," Cara says. "We should probably go. Maybe I'll see you again, though?"

"I hope so." Finn smiles warmly at her. I'm torn. I want Cara to move on from jerkface-of-the-year Jackson as soon as possible, but is this . . . too soon? The positive here is that Finn doesn't go to our school, so if things go sour, there's no chance of an awkward run-in. But the negative is that he belongs to a commune in the middle of nowhere, and the only way to see him is to come disrupt everyone's routines, which apparently is frowned upon. Also, how old is Finn? He looks pretty young, and I know most of them are, but if he's in his twenties, then I'm uncomfortable with the idea of he and Cara getting involved.

But I'm not her mom, so I guess it's not my call. Cara always knows what she's doing.

Part of me is relieved to be driving out of here. But part of me is actually a little sad not to stay longer. I can tell by the excitement on Cara's face that this is not going to be her last visit to the Haven. And as I look in the rearview mirror to the sight of Firehorse watching us go, I realize that I've got some serious shaping up to do if I don't want her to come alone.

EIGHT

When I get home, the card where Firehorse scrawled his web address starts to haunt me. It's been on my desk since the day I got it; I didn't have the heart to throw it away. I don't want to be a close-minded person. I don't want to ignore what Firehorse says just because he's weird and lives in a commune where no one is afraid of dock spiders.

Not only that, but if this is what Cara's into right now, if this is *all* she's into right now, I should try to be into it, too. At least a little.

So I pull my laptop out from underneath a couple shirts and a book, and I type in the address. At first glance, I really want to make fun of his website. Because it looks like he designed the site before I was born and hasn't changed the layout since. The font is papyrus. *Papyrus.* And underneath the heading is one of those thin lines in rainbow gradient. The background is gray bricks (which make the black font more than a little tough to see), and all the links are off to the left side in giant font on those blue rectangles that are supposed to look like buttons. It's so bad.

But I'm not here for the eyeball-murdering design. I'm here for the information. And the information is . . . well, there's a lot of it. There's so much, I get overwhelmed by it all. I start with the animal stuff, because that's what I dismissed the quickest before, knowing how Gavin felt about it already. But I don't want to be trained by the government to believe everything they tell me. I don't want to dismiss things just because my boyfriend has a tiny bit of experience in the area. Firehorse has all these facts laid out, and a million links to other websites. Reading it, taking it all in, I feel like I've been letting myself be misled my whole life.

After I'm done with that, I move on to some of the other tabs. His main point seems to be that we're lied to about a lot of things, and the true harm they're causing us. There's information about toxins in our foods and in the air, GMOs, electromagnetic fields, all kinds of stuff. According to Firehorse, the best way to rid your body of all these toxins and to stop harming the earth is to get away from society and live sustainably off the land—without harming animals and their habitats in the process. And that doing so doesn't just rid your body of toxins, but helps keep you safe from being spied on by the government, which he says we are, constantly, and in ways we don't even realize.

I'm not going to lie—some of this seems pretty crazy. The EMF stuff in particular; I really don't think my family's Wi-Fi is putting toxins into my body or stopping me from sleeping properly or making me less intelligent. But some of it . . . I don't know. I mean, he can't be wrong about all of this, can he? Especially not if Cara's into it. She's so smart.

During the car ride home today, she couldn't stop gushing about how good it makes her feel to go out there. How it makes her mind clearer. How eating vegan has made her body feel brand new. And who am I to say she's not on to something? Some people do feel better when they cut certain foods out of their diet. Some people don't have a choice, because of allergies or GI problems.

When my mom calls me down for dinner, I stare at the chunks of meat layered into the lasagna and feel a little ill. Both my parents dig into theirs without a second thought. I scrape the meat out of the center of my piece and take a bite instead that's just noodle and cheese. Except, crap, *cheese*. Wow, this veganism thing is going to be rough.

Mom notices my slow-motion chewing and furrows her brow at me. "Is something the matter? It tastes fine to me. I cooked it right, didn't I? It just had to go in the oven—I've done it plenty of times before."

She turns to my father for reassurance.

"Tastes great," he says. "It's hard to mess up the putting-it-in-the-oven part of the process, you know."

Mom turns back to me, smiling a little too proudly. "So, what's up?"

"Nothing, I just . . ." I hesitate. "I was thinking that maybe I want to become vegan."

Both of my parents crack up so hard. Dad actually has tears streaming down his cheeks by the time he stops laughing.

"I'm sorry, I don't see what's so funny," I say coolly.

"That wasn't a joke?" Mom asks.

"No. I've been reading some stuff, and I think it would be the right thing to do. For our environment *and* for the animals."

I can tell that Dad is still trying too hard not to laugh to even trust himself to speak, and I do not appreciate it.

Mom, however, comes to my aid. "If you really want to go vegan, Mailee, I'm all for it."

"Thanks, Mom." I smile at her.

"I'm not cooking you any of those weird soy burgers or anything, though. You're on your own there."

"I don't have to eat soy burgers, you know."

"What *are* you going to eat?" Dad asks with a smirk and a raised eyebrow.

"Food."

He laughs, but it's not as mirthful as it was before. "What's Gavin going to think about this?"

"He won't care." Well. He might care. I had honestly not thought about it, I only thought about Cara. But I know what Dad's doing. He wants me to talk myself out of this. Not happening, Dad.

I start to scrape the cheese out of my lasagna, too. Which really defeats the purpose of the lasagna, but oh well.

"Mailee, just eat it," Dad says gently. "You can start being a vegan tomorrow."

I should stand my ground. Should ignore the delicious smell wafting straight into my brain. But I can't. I'm starving and lasagna tastes amazing, so . . . I eat it. But I think about Firehorse the whole time, which pretty much ruins lasagna for me forever anyway.

Back in my room, I text Cara and casually insert mention of becoming vegan. Almost immediately, my phone rings.

"OH MY GOD," she practically screams. "I am so so so so so so happy you are doing this. I'm doing it, too. Everything Firehorse said was so . . . I mean I had never *thought* about things before! He knows so much."

"I know. I feel like kind of a jerk for not taking him seriously. He's done so much research."

"Do you think it's gonna be hard to be vegan when you're at theater camp?"

"I don't know. I haven't really thought about it. Worst-case scenario, I guess I'll be eating a lot of fruit." Theater camp is only six days away. I'm still bummed that Cara's not going, but I'm so excited about it anyway. This is going to be my last year, because next summer, I'm hoping to move to either California or New York, depending on where I get into school, and get myself acclimated and maybe/hopefully get a part in a play or something. Opportunities to do that aren't especially great here, so camp week is the only week I get to do anything, really, over the summer. I'm probably lucky Montana even *has* a theater camp. "Are you going to be okay for a week without me?"

"Of course. You don't need to worry about me, Mailee."

I don't want to bring up the breakup again, but I've definitely been worried and I want her to be okay.

"Well, if you need someone to talk to at all while I'm away, you know Gavin will be around."

"Mailee." She laughs. "I do have other friends, you know. Mostly the same friends you have. Gavin's nice and all, but we would definitely not hang out together if we didn't have you in common."

It's so strange to think about, but she's right. Gavin's become such a big part of my life that I forget he's not as big a part of my friends' lives. I could text him or call him if I was upset, and he'd make me feel better immediately. He might not know what to say to Cara. Or she might not want to hear it from him.

"Well, I'm just saying. Don't coop yourself up for the week. Make sure you get out."

"I'll be fine, I promise. I am sad about Jackson, obviously, but I know my life hasn't ended. He wasn't worth my time anyway."

I decide to test the waters. "Plus, I mean, there's Finn."

She pauses for a long moment. "Yeah, he's nice."

"How old is he?"

"Nineteen."

I guess that's okay.

"I was just talking to him, Mailee. I'm not planning to start dating anyone right now."

I flop down on my bed. "Think you'll go there while I'm away?"

"I don't know." She pauses again. "Probably. Would you be mad?"

"No, of course not. I'm just . . . I don't know. I feel like it was nice to visit, but I'm wondering how we fit, you know? Like, maybe I'll change some things and try to think about the environment more, but we don't live there, and I feel like, ultimately, they don't want it to be a place where people come and, like, hang out. They all seem to have roles. And I worry that we're kinda . . . interrupting?"

"Yeah, I get that. I probably would call before going again, not just show up. To make sure. You've gotta hand it to them, though, for how organized they are. Do you think Firehorse made them all a Book of Life Goals?"

I laugh. "If he did, it's definitely not as glorious as ours."

"Of course not. There's no way."

Cara has the Book of Life Goals at her house. She's the one who created it so she's the one who gets to keep it. Plus, let's face it, there's a good chance I'd accidentally lose it in my mess. That thing has been such a blessing for me. It helps me so much to see everything all laid out; my whole future.

And it helps Cara, too. Not in the same way, because she's so much less flighty than me, so much more serious. But she likes to see things laid out. She likes checking them off. Maybe this commune thing is a life experience she needs to check off before she can move on to the next thing.

NINE

Samantha and I will share a room at theater camp, as usual. Today, my mom brought us both shopping to get some things for our trip. I know it's super uncool, at age seventeen, to let your mom bring you shopping, but she promised to stay apart from us once we were in the mall. She just doesn't completely trust me not to buy anything frivolous with her credit card.

Theater camp is not roughing it, but I always bring a sleeping bag anyway because I don't trust the beds. I've had my old sleeping bag for too long and now the zipper's broken, so this year, I get a new one. Which means Samantha and I are in one of those outdoorsy stores with all the guns and camo outfits and plastic deer and fishing poles.

"Look at *this*," says Sam, holding up a gigantic pair of rubbery overalls with boots attached.

"Wow. You'd look beautiful in that."

"I know, right?" She tosses her curls and pretends to be a model. Then checks out the price tag. "Mailee, can you believe that this thing costs three hundred fifty dollars? How are these *possibly* worth that much?"

A man who's looking at something similar at the other end of the row scowls at us, and we both stifle giggles.

"Maybe we should just find the camping section," I suggest.

Samantha grudgingly puts the overalls back, but she can't stop herself from hugging a plastic deer before we leave the hunting-and-fishing section.

"Do you ever feel like you're not a true Montanan?" she asks. "All that wildlife-gear crap is so completely foreign to me. It's, like, how can we not even have collided with that world at all in seventeen years of living here?"

"I guess we're too suburban," I say, pausing to run my hand over a pair of fleecy socks that look incredibly soft. "But we collide with it a *little*, I think. I mean, Gavin hunts and stuff with his dad. And I've patted a baby cow on his ranch."

"That's what I'm talking about, though. How has it taken you *seventeen years* to pet a baby cow?"

"That is a very good point. I don't know how it's their fault, exactly, but I think I'm going to blame my parents for this one."

"Good call. I'm going to blame mine, too."

We reach the camping supplies, and Samantha cannot stop herself from diving into one of the tents they have on display. It doesn't *say* not to go in, but I look around guiltily before I follow her. We sit opposite each other, cross-legged.

This is a pretty big tent, but it still feels so . . . stifling. I remember Alexa saying how often the commune members at the Haven go camping. I don't get how they stand it. What if it rains? Are you *really* protected from a serious rainstorm by just this thin sheet of fabric? And what if the ground's uneven underneath your tent? Sleeping would be so uncomfortable.

"Hey, how's Cara doing?" Sam asks. "Seems like she's always busy when I call or text. I know she and Jackson broke up and everything, but . . ."

"She's doing okay, I think. We went back to that commune again, and she flirted with a guy there. So that's something."

"You went back there? I thought it was horrible the first time."

"It wasn't *horrible*. Gavin really hated it. I was kinda skeptical. But Cara loved it. She actually went a second time without me, so this was her third visit." I keep pretending this doesn't bother me, but it does. "Their leader is weird and intense, but I don't know. I think he's also pretty smart and educated. They all seem happy and they have jobs that have to get done and they have schedules, and you know Cara. You can see why she'd be drawn to that."

"I can. But you?" She raises an eyebrow at me.

"I know, I know. She does a lot for me, though. Felt like returning the favor wouldn't be the worst."

I don't tell Samantha about how I decided to become vegan, because I haven't told anyone yet except Cara and my parents, and I feel like I have to make it longer than one day as a vegan before I start announcing it.

"That's pretty nice. Especially considering how you feel about nature."

The tent flap opens and an employee scowls at us. "You aren't supposed to play in the tents," he says.

"Sorry," we both reply in unison, and vacate.

"Can't believe you got us in trouble," I mutter under my breath, even as I throw her a small smile. Cara's been so serious lately. I forgot what it feels like to have uncomplicated fun.

"Can't take me anywhere." She grins back, broadly.

"I know, how do I keep forgetting that?" I search through the sleeping bags for one that's pretty cheap but that doesn't feel like sandpaper, while Sam peeks casually inside another display tent, her expression daring the employee to come scold her again.

"This sleeping bag looks comfortable," she says, pointing to the interior of the tent. "Maybe you should come test it out."

"If you get us kicked out of this store before I manage to buy a sleeping bag, my mom will not be amused."

"But *I'll* be amused." She grins again.

God, why haven't I been hanging out with Sam more this summer? She's so easy. So perennially Samantha. She's not touchy, not unpredictable. The same person she's always been. I hadn't realized how tired I've been feeling. How exhausted from trying to keep up with Cara's lightning-fast mood swings.

"You're staring," says Sam. "Please remember, I'm already taken."

I roll my eyes. "I was just thinking that I'm really glad we're friends."

"Aw." She comes over and hugs me, a quick squeeze. "I'm glad, too."

And then the guilt kicks in. Not because I didn't mean what I said. I do; I'm very glad we're friends. But it's why I said it, why I was thinking it.

Because Cara is work right now. It's awful of me to resent that. I've *always* been work. Always. Except this summer, really. I've been pretty low maintenance this summer. And Cara's been quite the opposite.

We're probably about due for the swap, honestly.

"Hey, Mailee." Sam's voice is suddenly kind of serious. "I know Cara's feeling down and I do think it's nice that you went with her to this commune, but don't let yourself get too sucked in, okay?"

"What do you mean?" I furrow my brow.

"I mean . . . you're a people pleaser. Which isn't a bad thing. I am, too. Just don't let her feelings take so much priority over yours that you end up doing something you're uncomfortable with. Does that make any sense?"

"Yeah. It does, I guess."

She's right that I'm a people pleaser. I think that's a pretty common personality trait of actors, to be honest. You want people to like you and be happy with you, it's all part of the package. But I don't think that I let other people's feelings take precedence over mine. In fact, a lot of the time, I'm worried that I'm actually kind of selfish. I let Cara *clean my room* for me, and I can justify it all I want, but it's still . . . a little lazy. A little selfish. I don't think any harm can come from a few visits to a commune. To eating more vegetables and less steak. It's not my turn right now, it's hers.

She's my best friend, after all, and she's totally worth it.

Gavin stops by unexpectedly the next morning. He texted me when he was outside that his mom had sent him to the store and he didn't have a lot of time, but he wanted to see me since he was already passing by. I'm dressed and I'm wearing a little bit of makeup, so I figured I was presentable enough and told him to come on up to my room.

Gavin is a ridiculously loud walker. I can hear his footsteps from the moment he comes in the front door, all the way up the stairs and down the hall. He peeks his head into my open doorway and grins at me.

"What are you eating there?" Gavin points to the container of soy ice cream sitting next to me at my desk.

I make a face at the container. Which I've been doing for about fifteen minutes already. "Ugh, it's soy ice cream. *Not* as good as the real thing, let me tell you."

"Uh, yeah. I'd imagine not. Ice cream was not meant to be made out of plants."

He kisses me, long and lingering. Who needs ice cream, soy or regular, when you could kiss a handsome boy instead?

"So are you gonna tell me *why* you're eating soy ice cream?"

He plops down onto my bed, and I swivel my desk chair to face him. Here's a conversation I haven't been looking forward to.

"I . . . well, Cara and I both decided to try, um, being vegan."

His face is utterly expressionless. I'm pretty sure I just killed a part of him with my words. "Do I dare ask why?"

"Well, you know we went back to the commune again the other day. And I . . . I had a conversation with Firehorse about open-mindedness. So I looked at his website, and there was just . . . some pretty compelling and horrifying stuff. And I felt like maybe I don't want to . . ." I trail off because there is no way to end that sentence that won't offend this ranch-dwelling boy.

He must be exerting tremendous willpower because his voice is not a decibel off normal when he says, "Can I see what convinced you?"

"Yeah. I mean, there was a bunch of stuff, but . . ." I swivel back around and type the address into my laptop. Gavin stands behind me with his hands on the back of my chair.

"Wait, *this* is his website?" he says derisively. "Mailee, this looks like the first website ever made."

"I know. It's awful. But try to get past the hideousness and just . . . look at this video, Gavin." I show him a video of the cows tromping sadly through mud. "I mean, I know *your* family treats your animals well, but—"

"Don't let yourself get sucked in like this, Mailee. This is the worst kind of propaganda, because it tricks you if you don't know better. Look." He pauses the video with a click of my laptop's trackpad, and then moves the cursor to point at the ears of the cow. "She's not miserable, like the caption says. Her ears are pricked forward, her eyes are bright. She's happy. And see?" He unpauses it again. "They're all frolicking. They're excited, having fun. There's no context here at all, so I can't say for sure what's going on, but these animals are not suffering. It's probably spring and they're excited that they get to be outside."

My stomach sinks. God, I was so easily taken in. Gavin's totally right. If you look closely at the cows, they don't look upset, they don't look beaten down or sick. They look enthusiastic and healthy, just a little bit muddy. But the video's caption said they were suffering. It's what I was told, so it's what I saw. I feel so dumb, and the defensive part of me wants to fight back a little. Wants to be right.

"But what about the ones who don't get to go outside at all?"

"I don't have all the answers. But something I've heard my dad say every time he gets fired up about people being jerks to farmers and ranchers is that unhappy, unhealthy cows don't produce high-quality beef or as much milk. Your animals aren't healthy, your product isn't good. Plus, think about how much time and effort farmers put in every day. Out in the cold, in the rain, in the heat. Sure, there's always going to be monsters, but do you think most people are willing to put in that much work if they don't care about the animals at all?"

"No," I say in a small voice. I *feel* small. "But Firehorse said that sometimes people who are inside the industry can't see the problems. I mean . . ."

Gavin's jaw works. "Does it make any sense that Firehorse, or any random person on the Internet for that matter, would know more about farming than an actual farmer? If you research how rockets work, does that make you more of an expert than someone who builds them?"

I furrow my brow because he's being a *little* meaner than he needs to be, even though I get his point.

"I'm sorry," he says quietly. "It's not up to me to decide what you should or shouldn't eat. But I'm not gonna lie, Mailee, the reasoning behind it . . . it's hard not to take it personally. And I really think this guy is trying to manipulate you. It's gross."

I narrow my eyes. "Is it not also manipulative for my boyfriend to tell me I'm hurting his feelings by not eating meat?"

He runs a hand roughly through his hair. "I don't know. Maybe. I'm not trying to. I just want you to look at other websites besides *his* website, okay? Make your own choice. And remember that experts are experts. They know what's wrong, what needs to be fixed. They're not ignoring it. They're doing their best."

"You're right. You are. I just got really fired up. God, am I that easy to convince about things?"

"If you weren't, I'd never have gotten you to go out with me," Gavin says with a mischievous smile.

I tilt my head like I'm contemplating this. "True. I mean, there is definitely *zero* reason I should be dating you. You must've tricked me into it somehow."

He laughs and bends to kiss me. "I've gotta go home. Call me later?"

"We'll see." I smirk.

He leaves with a fake pout that could almost rival Cara's, and as soon as he's gone, I open up my web browser and search for more information about meat and dairy and all of it. Even the stuff about electromagnetic fields, which I was skeptical about to begin with. I read as much as I can find, pro and con, and vow not to let myself get coerced into a belief by a single source ever again.

I remember what Sam said yesterday about my people pleasing, and I feel like a mess inside. Like I'm being pulled in all of these directions. I don't want to be part of that freaking commune. But I *do* want them all to like me, to accept me.

And I don't want Cara to feel alone, especially not right now with the anniversary of Harper's death approaching. And I *also* don't want Gavin to be disappointed in me. His opinion matters almost as much to me as Cara's. No matter what I do, I'm going to see one of their faces let down.

But neither of them is the key to this. It's Firehorse. Thinking back to the language he used, it was totally manipulative. He made me feel like I was being a close-minded jerk for not listening to what he had to say. And he implied that people who are actual experts at something know less because they're too invested in the thing they're an expert at. How did I fall for that?

For dinner, Mom cooks a steak. And I eat the crap out of it.

TEN

My week at theater camp turns out to be basically the best ever, and I cannot wait to tell Cara about it. She's leaving Tuesday for her family's annual vacation, and I want to talk to her before then. Her family vacations are predictably awful; her parents basically hate each other now and I don't know why they force themselves to endure a whole week together every single summer. Not only that, but the trip now coincides very closely with the anniversary of Harper's death. Personally, I think it'd be best for everyone if they each grieved separately instead of in forced togetherness.

Anyway, Cara will inevitably come back miserable and depressed, and there won't be room for my theater camp gushing then. I want to do it now so that when she comes back, I can focus on helping to cheer her up.

She agrees to hang out, but it takes her a lot longer than usual to respond to my texts. I wonder if she's getting pre-depressed for her trip. I couldn't blame her if she was. On my way to her house, I stop by the store for some ice cream. Mint chocolate chip is her favorite; she can never withstand its charms.

I let myself into her house, like I always do. Her parents are at work, so I don't have to make awkward small talk with either (or, God forbid, both), and I drop off the pint of ice cream in the freezer before I head upstairs, in case I need to produce it later for a surprise cheer-up.

Cara's in her room, exactly where I expected her to be. Her house is bigger than mine, and so is her bedroom. And because everything in here is so organized, it looks even bigger. There's no clutter, no clothes strewn across the floor, nothing. She has a few posters on the wall, but they're arranged decoratively, not thrown up wildly like mine are. Her bed is made, her desk is organized, and she's sitting in the corner, reading a book.

"Hey!" she says, but doesn't look up.

Whatever she's reading cannot possibly be that interesting. I suppress a flash of irritation.

"Did you miss me?" I ask cheerfully.

"Of course." She marks her page and slowly lowers the book to her lap. "Did you have fun?"

"So much. I was worried since this is my last summer that it wouldn't live up to my expectations, but oh man. It was so great. The best year so far, hands down. This fall is going to be *amazing*. Can you believe it's almost our senior year?"

Her face breaks into a tentative smile at my enthusiasm. "I can't believe it at all."

"Everything we've worked for, all coming together."

Her smile fades. "Yeah."

"Hey, are you all right?" I sink onto her bed. Maybe I shouldn't have gushed so hard about camp. Maybe she regrets that she didn't come. A stab of guilt pierces me. I'm starting to really hate feeling this way around her all the time.

"Of course. Yeah, I'm fine. Just thinking about, you know, Harper and stuff."

"I'm sorry." I vacate my spot on the bed, and instead join her in her big leather armchair. This was easier when we were younger. We could both fit in the seat. But as we've gotten taller and developed hips, we've had to adjust. I sit on the arm with my feet beside her in the seat of the chair. I wrap my arms around her like I've done every time she's been sad in this room for the past decade. She rests her head against the side of my leg, but no tears fall. She looks hollowed out. It feels like I'm hindering, not helping.

"I like your necklace," I say, trying to get her mind onto something else. "Is it new?"

"Thanks." She touches her fingertips to the pendant. "Alexa suggested it to me. It helps protect against toxic frequencies and stuff."

Toxic . . . frequencies?

"That's neat," I say. "What are toxic frequencies?"

She pulls back and gazes up at me. "I thought you read Firehorse's website?"

"I did, but—*oh*. Like from Wi-Fi and stuff?"

"Yeah. Wi-Fi, phones, other technology. Probably in places we don't even know about. It's hard to avoid it if you're not, you know, up in the mountains, but this helps. It makes me feel . . . I'm sure you'll think it's crazy, but I honestly feel healthier since I've started wearing this. Like my brain is lighter."

"That's good."

I don't know what else to say. I'm glad she's feeling healthy, but this has got to be some kind of serious placebo effect. Does she want me to ask where she got it so I can wear one, too? I'm . . . not going to do that.

An awkward silence grows between us. I have never been good with awkward silences. Or silences in general. My brain screams at me to blurt out something, *anything*, for the sake of putting noise back into the room.

"I brought you some mint chocolate chip ice cream," I tell her.

She looks at me like I'm an idiot. "I can't eat that."

"What? Why not?"

She sighs. "Did you forget that being a vegan means no dairy?"

"Oh, right. I forgot about that."

"Yeah. I'm guessing your vegan diet didn't last too long, then?"

Of course. We haven't talked about this at all. I didn't even think to mention it in the wake of my departure preparations before camp.

"No, I decided to do some more research into it," I tell her. "Turns out, some of the stuff on that website was misleading. I'm not saying that there's nothing at all valid in deciding not to eat meat and stuff, but I decided that for me, when I had looked at all the evidence . . . I disagree with Firehorse's take on it. So I'm going to keep eating meat and dairy."

I know before I've finished talking that she's mad. Her eyes practically burn holes into my face.

"So you're saying I'm an idiot who didn't do any research, basically?" Her tone is even, but it's like being stared in the face by a venomous snake. It hasn't struck yet, but you know it's just waiting for you to move.

"Obviously I wasn't saying that! I'm just—I decided not to do it, that's all." I take a deep breath and decide to go for broke, honesty-wise. "I don't think Firehorse is wrong about every-thing, but I also think that he's overdramatizing when he says that the government is propagandizing us, and that we're all ignorant. I mean, maybe they're trying, who knows. It's not like our government is so great right now. But we have the Internet and stuff. We can talk to people from all over and make up our own minds. And I feel like by giving us that totally biased web-site, Firehorse was doing exactly what he says the government does. I'm sorry, Cara, I know you like his ideas, and that's fine. But I think he's manipulative."

She explodes out of the chair, crossing her arms furiously. "*He's* manipulative? Let's be real, Mailee, who convinced you not to be vegan? Gavin couldn't *possibly* have had anything to do with it, could he?"

"He didn't—only a little. He didn't tell me not to, he just pointed out some of the things in those videos that were lies. And he told me to do my own research."

She's hitting on something I'm already worried about—*did I let my boyfriend manipulate me the same way she's letting Firehorse manipulate her?*—and it infuriates me. The two feel very different. Gavin has a personal stake in this, but that doesn't mean he doesn't know what he's talking about. He didn't tell me I couldn't make my own decision. He just told me I should look at it from all sides. And I did. I really did. Besides, I don't *want* to give up meat and dairy and eggs. I love those things. It should be up to me what I eat or don't eat, not some guy who lives in the woods.

"Exactly. If you want to talk emotional manipulation, it's your boyfriend who *lives on a ranch* telling you not to listen to Firehorse. I've done my research, too, you know." She clutches at her necklace, and I hold my tongue because I don't want to be fighting and any criticisms I make about that thing are only going to worsen all this. I'm not an expert, either. Anything I say is opinion, just like anything Cara says. "Firehorse isn't wrong. Do you even know how messed up everything is in our world right now? We are heading down a really bad path, and Firehorse is not the enemy here. Why can't you see that?"

"I don't know," I say honestly. "I can see how messed up the world is. It's just . . . the more you think about stuff he says, the more you seem to be totally into what he's saying. And that's fine. But for me, the more I've thought about the things he says, the less they make sense to me. I guess we just aren't going to agree on this."

Her eyes fill with tears. "I guess we're not."

"Let's change the subject," I plead. This argument is making my stomach hurt.

"I think I actually want to be alone right now." Cara's voice quivers, but the rest of her is steady.

"But—"

"I'll call you after I'm home from my trip. Once I feel settled back in."

"Cara. This was by far not our worst fight. And now—"

"The fact that you think this is not our worst fight just proves how much I need you to get out of my room right now."

"I—"

"Now."

I guess there's nothing for me to do but leave. Feeling like I'm trapped in a nightmare, I slide off the chair and head unsteadily for the door. My eyes sting and I'm shaking.

"And take the ice cream," she says icily, just as I'm passing through her doorway. "Please."

Part of me expects her to come after me, stop me before I've left the house. I open the freezer loudly so she knows I'm still here, and do the same when I open—and close—her front door. Nothing. When I get to my car, I turn back for a moment, look toward her window. She's not there. Not even watching me leave.

I don't understand why she's this mad. I am completely blindsided by what just happened between us. She said she would call me after she gets back from her trip, and I really hope that, despite her tone, she will. If she doesn't, I'll call her. I'll beg for her forgiveness for whatever it is that I did wrong here.

I cry the entire way home, because this doesn't feel like a fight at all.

This feels like a breakup.

ELEVEN

I'm a moping mess for the next couple days. My emotions journal gets several new entries about different kinds of sadness and angst. Gavin tries to cheer me up, but I'm irrationally mad at him, as though he somehow caused this with his reasonableness. I don't want him to know how irrational I'm being, though, so when he invites me over on Wednesday, I go.

His family's ranch is a beautiful place. The house is log, with a big stone fireplace, and the barn is red with one of those arched roofs—a total barn stereotype. Though there are also some other barn-like structures out behind it that aren't as picturesque. But with the fields that go on and on and on, where the cows roam, the place is like something from a storybook.

Gavin's mom is heading into their house when I arrive, a bucket full of blackberries clutched in one hand. She gives me a friendly wave with the other, which I return.

"Gavin's in the barn," she says, and then continues indoors.

I like Gavin's mom. She's very nice, but she's not much of a talker. Part of me thinks it's that she doesn't see me as a long-term prospect for her son. He's going to stay here and take over the ranch, and I'm going to move to a big city far away. Which is something I've shoved deep into the back pocket of my brain; lately, it's the absolute last thing I want to think about. When I think about the future with Gavin, I'm deluding myself that we can totally make it work long distance when the time comes.

My boyfriend is easy enough to find; he's standing in what they refer to as the "hospital"—which is just a series of pens that hold cows who need special attention. His forearms rest on the top bar of the metal gate in front of the pen, and he's watching a cow within.

When he sees me, he greets me with a smile and a kiss.

"What's going on here?" I ask.

"She's having a baby." He points to the back end of the cow (not usually the part of a cow I want to look at) and sure enough, there are tiny hooves sticking out of there.

"Well *that* doesn't look fun." I wrinkle my nose.

Gavin laughs. "I suspect it's not."

We both watch the cow in silence for a few minutes. It's not real exciting, to be honest. She's mostly just lying there.

"How're you doing?" Gavin asks.

"I'm okay." I grip the red-painted metal bar in front of me. I promised myself that I *would* be okay today. But I'm a little shaky.

"Are you?" Gavin presses.

The cow lets out a grunt of unhappiness and I'm inclined to agree with her. Tears sting my eyes and I blink them back fiercely.

"Today's the anniversary of Harper's death," I say. "It's just . . . getting to me more than I expected. With Cara mad at me and everything. Last year I was so focused on helping Cara through it, I didn't have much time to, like, sit and think about everything. I don't know. Harper was a big part of my life, too. It's been—it's just not easy, sometimes. She was six years old. It's so unfair."

Gavin pulls me to his chest. He doesn't say anything, which I appreciate. Words don't fix this kind of thing, no matter how well meaning. I let him hold me until I feel calm again.

"Can we stay here and watch this calf be born?" I ask. "I've never seen anything be born before."

"Sure, if that's what you want to do. I've gotta warn you, though, sometimes it takes a while."

He looks pleased that I'm interested. It feels pretty nice to actually please someone for a change.

More of the calf is showing now; its nose and forelegs peek out. Gavin explains that this is the part that sometimes takes a while, and once the rest of the head comes out, the rest of the calf will follow soon after. The cow is being impressively chill about this situation, in my opinion. She definitely doesn't seem happy about what's going on, and can't seem to decide if she wants to stand or lie down, but she's handling it like a pro.

"I hope Cara's doing okay," I say, because I can't get out of my own head. "On her vacation. Last year she came back from that trip so broken."

And last year I helped her through it. But this year . . . I'm afraid she won't even let me try.

"Maybe . . ." Gavin pauses. "Listen, I really hate that I'm about to say this, but maybe all this new stuff she's into will help her handle everything this year. The placebo effect can be a pretty strong thing."

I think of Cara's new necklace, protecting her from toxins or whatever. "I guess. I hope so." I tap my nails on the metal bar. Part of me secretly hopes not. So that she needs me. I'm awful. "Do you think she's done with me?"

"What? That's a ridiculous question, Mailee."

"Is it?"

Gavin reaches for my hand. "I haven't known Cara very long, but I know your friendship isn't one-sided. And maybe I don't know what's going on with her this summer, but the problem's not you. I promise."

I wish that made me feel better. But there's more to it, things I can't say to Gavin because he's my boyfriend and he doesn't need to know how desperately insecure I am deep inside. How much I need gestures, overt signs, to know how much a person likes me, or else I'm forever questioning it. Even Cara. Especially Cara. She's prettier than me, smarter, better. I've been waiting our whole friendship for her to realize it and I'm starting to worry that the day has finally come.

"She thinks she needs this new diet and this protection from air toxins and the firm schedule of that commune, but she doesn't," I tell him. "She needs to talk about what's wrong and actually *fix* it instead of covering it up with this stuff." I feel like a bitter hag talking about Cara like this, but it's true. She's not dealing.

"Hey, it's happening." Gavin points to the cow, and I turn my attention back to the pen.

A newborn calf comes sliding into the world, slimy but adorable. The cow stands up and starts aggressively licking it clean. The calf tries to stand, too, but its legs aren't quite steady yet.

"You know what, it's pretty nice to see new life come into the world today," I say. Watching the little calf with its mom makes me feel better in a way that talking about things hasn't. Who even knows why. "I'm sorry, though. I feel like I'm being a major downer."

"You're allowed," Gavin says, flashing me a heart-melting smile.

"I'm really lucky I have you."

He kisses me; the sort of kiss I feel all the way down to my toes.

"Not as lucky as I am," he says.

We kiss again, melding together, and it is one of those moments I know is going to stick with me, because it feels so perfect.

Until my phone rings, shattering the mood.

"It's Cara," I say, surprised. Gavin nods encouragingly and I step away to answer it.

"Can you come over?" Her voice is weak, heavy with tears.

"Come over? Where are you?"

"I'm home. I pretended to have a stomach virus yesterday so my parents would go without me. Can you just come over?"

"Yeah, of course. I'll be there in a few."

We hang up, and I turn to Gavin. "Cara didn't go on her vacation, and she needs me to go over to her house, I guess."

He nods again, less enthusiastic this time. I know he's disappointed that I'm leaving, and that makes me feel terrible. But I can't ignore a phone call from my sobbing best friend, can I?

"I'll call you after?" I say in a small voice.

"Yeah, sounds good." His smile is warm, but tiny.

Before I go, I kiss him again, put my whole self into it. And it's nearly impossible to tear myself away.

Cara's not in her bedroom when I get to her house, but I didn't expect her to be. She's in Harper's. About nine months ago, Cara's mom decided she couldn't stand leaving the room as it was anymore; she donated clothes and stuffed animals and toys, stored or threw away anything that was too damaged to donate. She repainted, and took down the drawings of dragons and princesses and wild animals that Harper had proudly displayed on the walls. And then she turned it into a guest room. That no one ever sleeps in.

Cara's sitting on the bed, which besides a single nightstand is the only piece of furniture in this barren, stale room. Her face is tear-streaked, her eyes swollen and red, but she isn't crying, not right now.

"I wasn't really ready to talk to you," she says, which isn't the greeting I wanted. "But I just . . . needed someone."

I swallow my pride and my insecurities and I go to her, because this is not the time to hash out whatever's going on between us. "What do you need me to do?" I ask, cautiously squeezing an arm around her shoulders.

"I don't know." She drops her face into her hands. "I couldn't stand to go through a whole vacation with my parents."

"I don't blame you." I bite my lip, trying to come up with something good to say. Something healing. Something even remotely helpful. "I've been kind of sad today, too. I can only imagine how it must feel for you."

She looks up at me, almost perplexed. "You feel sad about it, too?"

"Of course. She may not have been my sister, but she was in my life for a really long time, Cara."

"Wow." She wipes her cheek with the back of her hand. "Honestly, I think I needed to hear that from someone. Like, that I'm not the only one who misses her. My parents have done such a good job this year erasing every bit of her from our lives. We don't even have any pictures of her on the *walls* anymore."

I squeeze my arm around her even tighter, a knot untying in my chest. I said the right thing, somehow, and maybe I'm starting to mend us.

"You can always talk to me about her," I say. "You can talk to me about anything, you know that."

Her expression sours. This time, I said the wrong thing. "Not *anything*."

She closes her fist around that pendant she's wearing.

"We can still *talk* about anything even if we don't agree on every last detail," I say, trying to sound gentle rather than frustrated.

"I wanted to go to the Haven today," she says, not looking at me. "But they go out foraging on Wednesdays, so no one's there."

Jealousy rises up, sick and ugly in my stomach. What could *they* do for her that I can't? "Well, I'm here," I say. "And we can do anything you want."

"I want to go see Avalon," she says softly.

And the puzzle pieces all click into place. "Avalon's not Harper," I say gently.

That was not just the wrong thing to say—it was the *most* wrong thing to say.

"I know that." Her voice is pure ice. "When are you going to stop acting like I'm delusional, Mailee?"

I edge away from her. "I'm not! That's not what I'm doing at all. I'm just *saying*, you can't replace Harper with Avalon. It's not going to make you feel better."

"I'm not *replacing* her," Cara snarls. "God, Mailee, you are just not getting this at all."

"Clearly not." I stand up, because I feel like I'm going to cry and I don't need her to see it.

"What are you doing?"

I take a deep breath and turn back bravely to face her. "I'm leaving. Because I'm not going to sit here and fight with you today. It's not what either one of us needs."

For about two seconds, I feel really mature and brave and right.

And then Cara says, "Fine. But don't come crawling to me tomorrow with an apology thinking everything will be fixed. In fact, don't call me at all. I'll call you when I'm ready. *If* I'm ready."

I swallow hard, but I don't say anything in response. I just leave.

TWELVE

This has been the longest week and a half of my life. Cara and I have never gone this many days without speaking. It's quite honestly a miracle that I've managed to keep from calling her, and I've only succeeded because every time I have the urge, I text Gavin instead with some variation of, Has it been long enough? Should I call her?? He always tells me not to. Patiently.

On that note, it's also a miracle that Gavin hasn't killed me yet.

Right now, I'm at Samantha's house, sitting on her bedroom floor. Margaret is here, too, and together they are a terrible influence on me.

"Gavin is wrong," says Sam. "No offense to him, but he's, like, always polite. And he totally does not understand the intricacies of female friendships."

"So you think I should call Cara? She said not to. And she was pretty mad the last time I saw her. The last *two* times I saw her."

"You *need* to call her," says Margaret. "She's probably embarrassed now about how bad she overreacted and figures you've been festering about it and is afraid to call you."

Cara would never be afraid to call. I actually think Gavin's right; Cara was so angry and so firm before. I don't think she'd want me to call. But I really, really want to. It's the worst when the thing you want to do and the thing you should do aren't matching up.

"All right. I'm gonna do it." I pull out my phone and stare apprehensively at its screen. "Maybe I should text her instead?"

"No," they say firmly, in unison.

"Fine," I grumble, and make the call before I can talk myself out of it.

They're both watching me intently, like I'm a reality TV show, and I wish I'd waited till I was alone to do this. Especially when it rings four times with no answer. Cara never lets my calls ring this many times. On the fifth ring, she answers.

"Didn't I say *I'd* call *you*?" is what she says. Tersely.

"You did, but . . . you haven't." My voice is weak. I feel pathetic. "I know you're mad at me, Cara, but if we don't talk about it, nothing's going to get fixed."

"Maybe it shouldn't get fixed. Maybe we're growing apart."

Sam's eyes widen and now I *really* wish we were having this conversation alone, or at least out of hearing range.

"Since when?" I demand. "We were fine until I said one thing about Avalon and—"

"Look, I just need some space, Mailee. I need to figure out what's important to me and what I want without being so wrapped up in . . . what someone else wants."

"But we already have the plan, in the Book of Life Goals."

"Maybe I don't want that plan, though!" she bursts out. "Maybe I don't have the exact same dreams I had in seventh grade, and maybe I'm tired of feeling like I'm supposed to."

"Why haven't you ever said anything like that before, then?" I huddle into myself and try not to look at Samantha or Margaret, who are definitely regretting this suggestion.

"Because you're so obsessed with that stupid book, Mailee. And I'm not—" Her voice breaks a little. "I'm not, like, trying to stop being your friend. I just need to extricate myself a little, you know? I feel like our personalities have gotten totally entangled in each other and I need to pull back for a while."

"Okay." I'm struggling to hold back tears. It's like she stabbed me a million times with a knife. "If that's what you want."

"I *will* call, okay? Just . . . give me a little time."

I hang up and press my face into my knees. Within moments, there are two pairs of arms around me, but I feel cold.

"I'm so sorry," Samantha says. "I don't think either of us would have suggested you call her if we *ever* thought she'd say anything like that."

"Did I do something wrong?" I ask pathetically, peering up over my knees. My eyes are burning, but tears don't fall. "Am I, like, the world's most overbearing friend?"

"You're a great friend," Sam reassures me. "We all know Cara's going through some stuff. Maybe you're . . . an easy outlet to blame."

I want this to comfort me, but it doesn't. "I'm really sorry, you guys, but I think I just want to go home."

They're understanding, of course, because it's hard not to be understanding when someone has just gotten dumped by their best friend, and pretty soon I find myself alone in my bedroom, sitting on the floor in the middle of a pile of clothes.

It's that stupid commune that's pulling Cara away from me, I know it is. But I also have to wonder if I'm entirely blameless. I am a good friend, or at least I try to be. But do I take more than I give? Am I too much work?

These are insecurities I've had forever. Acquaintances come and go, but Cara, I thought she'd be there forever. She *wanted* to create the Book of Life Goals. She had so much fun decorating it and writing bullet points and schedules in her perfect, bubbly handwriting. We updated it at the end of the school year, and she was still into it then. Now I wonder if she felt forced into it, if she was faking. If she's such a good friend and human being that she stuck by me when I annoyed the crap out of her, and now I've finally taken her too far over the edge.

That can't be true, though. I'm not perfect, but am I so awful? I don't think so. I hope not. I'll give Cara space for a little while, like she asked, and then when she's ready, I'll try harder.

I look around my room. It'll never be as clean as Cara's, not without her help. But it is not endearing to be this sloppy. I can do so much better. If Cara's going to figure out some things about herself, I should do the same thing.

So I scoop up all the clean clothes off my floor, and I start to fold.

Fall

THIRTEEN

When things end, there's supposed to be a reason. A catalyst. Something you can look back on later when you need an explanation. Even if it doesn't make you feel any better.

But right now, in the fall of my senior year, I am losing my best friend for no reason at all. It's like the two of us are held together by an old, fraying rubber band. One wrong move and it could break from anywhere.

Senior year is supposed to be the pinnacle of my existence so far. A glorious culmination of high school. And it's supposed to be happening with Cara by my side. Every morning, I wait in our spot, not knowing if she'll show. Or if she'll even hang out with me if she does. Her greetings are usually brief and impersonal. Sometimes she stays, especially if other friends are around, but more often she goes on ahead into school without me.

Ever since she told me that she needed space, things haven't been the same. We went from best friends to close acquaintances. I guess the amount of space she needed could fill a galaxy. But I haven't given up, and since we've been back at school, I wait for her steadfastly every morning until my phone says 8:25; exactly five minutes until I have to be in homeroom.

Our spot is beneath one of the sycamore trees that decorate the yard of our high school. There's nothing special about this particular tree, we just claimed it one day sophomore year. Meeting here became part of our routine.

Today, a balled-up sweatshirt protects my butt from the dew-slicked ground as I sit with my back against the tree, alone, scrolling mindlessly through social media stuff on my phone. The tree's not far from the school's entrance, and every day that Cara doesn't show, I swear I can feel the pitying looks from both friends and people I don't know as I start my solo walk of shame into the building. I'm *imagining* the pitying looks, Samantha says. Maybe she's right, I don't know.

A backpack thunks down beside me, but it doesn't belong to Cara. It belongs to Gavin. He sits on the backpack, probably smooshing his homework into a wrinkled mess. It took years for Cara to get me to put my homework neatly in a folder like she does, and never hand in wrinkled, smudged, halfhearted work. Seeing him sit on his backpack like that would drive her nuts. But she's not here, so I guess it doesn't matter. She would be proud of me, though. My room won't be featured in a home décor magazine anytime soon, but I've managed to keep it clean all by myself for months now.

"Good morning," Gavin says cheerfully, and kisses me on the cheek. "I brought you coffee."

He hands me a steaming Styrofoam cup. I inhale the scent of perkiness gratefully. Perkiness smells vaguely of pumpkin, as it turns out.

"You are my hero," I tell him.

"You're setting the bar for hero a little low, don't you think?"

I laugh. "Maybe don't complain, though, when it works in your favor."

He scarfs down a doughnut, his gaze wandering. "No Cara today, huh?"

"Not yet, but she'll definitely be here today."

He frowns. It's not the displeased kind of frown so much as the *I want to say something but don't want to hurt your feelings* kind of frown. I take an extra big gulp of my coffee, and it burns its way to my stomach.

"She will," I insist, even though he didn't contradict me.

Everyone in drama club knows that today's the day they announce the stage manager. Cara missed it last week when they announced roles for the fall play—when they announced that *I* got the lead role—but she won't miss this.

Last week's announcement was my moment, but this week will be hers. It's the culmination of everything we've worked toward since seventh grade, everything we immortalized in the Book of Life Goals. We have big plans to be famous together and it's kind of hard to be famous together by myself. I know she is big in this figuring herself out notion, but this is *the* goal.

"I hope she is," he says, even though I know he only cares because I care. "But it's 8:20, so I'm going to head in and give you some alone time with your coffee."

I smile, even though it doesn't quite come easily. "Okay. I'll see you after drama club."

He kisses me once more, this time on the lips, and then he lopes off toward the building. Gavin is a lot fussier than me about timeliness. I wish he'd stay and wait with me longer, but I know he doesn't think I should bother waiting for Cara at all, so I guess I can only expect so much out of him.

The crowds of people hanging around out front of the school are starting to thin. Now it's mainly just the smokers and me.

I glance at my phone. 8:24. There's still time.

8:25. I hesitate, but no, today I'll give Cara a little longer. I won't go in just yet. She'll come.

8:26. It hurt, last week, that she wasn't there for my announcement. That she wasn't one of the people surrounding me and cheering when they called *my name* for the lead role. It put a damper on my daydreams, the visions of myself on a red carpet surrounded by paparazzi and reporters begging to know who I'm wearing. But I will be there for her announcement, because I want to show her how much this still matters. How much she needs to forget about the stupid commune and remember what's important.

8:27. I want to have our moment together, when I say something sappy and lame about how I couldn't have done it without her, how her support has been everything, her lists keeping me on track when I can barely put down a pencil without losing it. How much she deserves the stage manager position because she's the smartest, most organized person I know. It might be weird to get too heartfelt about this huge thing when I don't know if it even matters to her anymore, but I don't care. I'm going to do it anyway.

8:28. I heave a sigh and put my phone away. I can't wait any longer without getting into trouble, and my heart feels like dust.

Cara's going to miss this, too.

FOURTEEN

Cara is not named stage manager.

I should have expected this, maybe, but I am totally shocked. For five years, Cara's been the picture of dedication. It's been different this year, sure, but she's made it to . . . well, definitely more than half of our drama club meetings.

My stomach turns to lead. What do I do when she finds out she's not stage manager? She'll be crushed. Won't she?

Or will she just quit drama club altogether and spend even more time at the Haven, playing big sister to Avalon and pretending everything's normal?

"Mailee." Sam tugs on my arm. "We have to start rehearsal."

"Right." I try to shake free of the cloud in my head. "Just let me text Cara."

She sighs. "If you really want to. But, Mailee . . . you're not alone if you don't have her, you know. The rest of us aren't going anywhere."

I swallow a lump in my throat and force a smile. I'm an actress. I can fake it with the best of them. "Thank you. I appreciate that."

Samantha isn't Cara, but she's a great friend. We have a lot of fun together, and she's tried hard the past couple months to help fill the Cara-shaped hole in my chest.

I duck out into the hallway, and instead of sending Cara a text, I call her. If she's at the Haven—and let's face it, where else would she be?—she doesn't have service, but it's worth a try, anyway.

She answers. I'm strangely disappointed. If she's in cell range, why isn't she *here*?

"Hey, where are you?" I ask. My voice doesn't sound as nonchalant as I want it to.

"We came into town real quick to get supplies."

"What do you mean you came into town real quick? You *live* in town."

"Yeah, I know, but listen, I'm glad you called! I was going to call you in a little bit. There's gonna be a party at the Haven tomorrow night. A harvest celebration. Will you please, please come? You can drive out after school."

"So . . . you won't be at school tomorrow, either?"

She's silent for too long. "No."

"Cara—"

"Look, we can talk about all that later. It'd mean *so much* to me if you came to this party. It's going to be fun, I promise. I want us to spend time together again. I miss you."

I really do not want to say yes to the party. I like a good party as much as the next girl, but I have never been to a harvest celebration and it doesn't seem like my thing. Plus, I hate the Haven for messing up my senior year and taking away my best friend. If I'd known this would happen, I *never* would have gone the first time. Or the second time. I just couldn't have dreamed that Cara would become so attached to a place where you have to pee in an outhouse with questionable structural integrity.

But I *do* want to say yes to spending more time together. There are millions of books and articles and TV shows that tell you how much it sucks to go through a breakup with a boyfriend, but no one prepares you for the pain of the moment when your best friend stops needing you. And as bad as breakups can be, this feels much, much worse. I need her. More than I need Gavin or my parents or anyone. I need my best friend.

"Okay. I'll come." Honestly, I'm surprised the words come out of my own mouth. But maybe if I go, I can convince her to stop skipping drama club. There's still the spring play. She can be stage manager for that, if she gets it together. Before now, she's had such a good record. They'll remember that, they'll look back on this with understanding. I'm sure of it. "Of course I want to spend more time with you, too. That will never change."

"Good." Maybe I'm reading into it, but her voice sounds relieved. "I'll see you tomorrow, then. After school. You have no idea how much I'm looking forward to this, Mailee."

"Me too." It's only partly a lie.

Cara's always been my rock, my day planner, my life coach. Maybe now it's time for me to be hers.

"You want me to come with you to that thing tomorrow?"

Gavin is doing his homework while draped across my bed. I'm sitting in a tiger-striped beanbag chair, laptop on my knees. This has become our after-school routine. The reward for getting our homework done is kissing, and that's pretty much the best reward there is.

"You'd be bored out of your mind," I say. "I appreciate the offer, though."

"You're sure it's safe?" Worry flickers across his face, which is adorable. "You're going to be out in the woods overnight?"

"Cara will be there. It's just a bunch of hippies worshipping the moon or something."

"I'm pretty sure harvest celebrations are about crops, not the moon."

"Does it really matter?" I stick out my tongue.

"*Anyway.*" He shoots me an exasperated look. "I'm just saying. You don't have cell service there and it's so far out of the way. What if you have a medical emergency and—"

"It's not like it's a frat party or something. What kind of medical emergency could I possibly have?" I don't drink and Gavin knows it. It's one of the many things that makes my parents trust me, and like Cara said, if I'm going to break their trust, it's going to be for something really good.

Let's not mention that by telling them I'm spending the night with Cara but not telling them *where*, I'm breaking their trust a teeny bit. But it's not wrong, what I'm doing. If they do find out, they'll understand.

"You could still get hurt. What if you fall into a fire or something? No one even knows you're going there except me and Cara."

"Okay, first of all. I am not going to fall into a fire. And second of all, let's say something horrible and tragic does happen. You wouldn't tell my parents where to find me?"

"Of course I would."

"Good. Problem solved, then."

He stares mutely at me for an awkwardly long moment, then says, "Okay. Point taken. I'll trust you not to fall in a fire. But I don't like the vibe that place has."

"I know you don't. Trust me, I will be back here the second I can tear Cara away from there."

If I can figure out how to tear her away. I keep flashing back to this summer, wondering how it got to this point in the first place. I'm suspicious that the groundwork was laid during Cara's second visit, when she went without me. That they made her feel like she belonged, that she was one of them. They instigated the fault line that's cracking the earth between us, and she's breaking away, just like they hoped she would. She's breaking away *hard*.

I am trying not to be judgmental of the people who live there. I genuinely believe that the idea behind it is nice. Maybe I'm just bitter because they recruited Cara and weren't interested in me at all. Maybe I'm vengeful because of the rift they caused between us. Maybe I'm ashamed because I couldn't last three days as a vegan and would have lasted even less if I'd tried to live in one of their shacks.

But something about that place bothers me. As much as I'd like to believe that the problem is all in my head, it just feels slimy. What have they done to hook Cara so deep? It's one thing for her to visit a bunch over the summer, but to keep going now that school's started? I don't understand it, and it feels wrong.

"Well, you'll definitely be back by Saturday afternoon, right?" Gavin asks while ferociously erasing a mistake in his lab notebook.

"Yeah, why?"

"I *know* you know Saturday's our six-month anniversary."

I arch an eyebrow. I did know, but I'm surprised he's bringing it up. "And you made plans for us?"

"Dinner reservation. I'll pick you up at 6:30."

"Really?" I know it's just dinner, but my heart melts into a puddle of slushy happiness.

"Yes, really. Besides, even if we didn't have an anniversary, we still haven't celebrated you getting the lead role in the play. I'm proud of you."

I close my laptop slowly. I don't know what to say.

So I don't say anything. I cross the room and I kiss him.

"Finally," he teases. "If I'm not going to see you again till Saturday, we definitely need to be making out more."

"You're such a dork." I loop my arms around his neck. "But I guess that's what I like about you."

He kisses me this time, and I can't help but think that it's too bad they can't bottle up kissing and sell it as a medicine. His mouth on mine makes all my problems disappear.

Tomorrow, I'll go to the harvest party and win Cara back from her weird commune friends. But tonight, I will feel nothing but happiness.

FIFTEEN

If I'm being real, driving to the Haven creeps the heck out of me. The road is such a mess and I cannot even let myself consider what I'd do if I broke down out here. No cell service. I'd have to walk *really* far. And I'm alone this time; no one to walk with me if it happens.

I clutch the steering wheel steady with sweaty fists and try to enjoy the scenery. The trees on either side of me, sloping up steep hills that turn into mountains. While I may not be a fan of the weird shacks and the lack of electricity and plumbing, I can't deny that they picked a great location for this place. The view during the drive is nice, and from the commune, it's breathtaking. Of course, with those breathtaking views come the breathtakingly large dock spiders. I'm sorry, I can't let go of the dock spider incident. I will never let go of it.

I'm nearly there, now, if I recall correctly. I've left civilization and pavement behind. Conifers have replaced buildings. Boulders have replaced billboards. My car bumps over stones that have become slowly exposed over time, with all the wear that this muddy barely-a-road has seen.

I slow to a crawl as the road continues to narrow; branches shriek as they scrape along my windows. I cringe. The mud is really thick right now, too. It's not what you'd expect this time of year, more like the kind of mud you see after spring rains. My tires spin slickly through it, spraying up globs of muck onto my side windows. And then it happens.

I turn a sharp corner . . . and my car just sinks.

It's like the car was on a platform and someone yanked it out. Or maybe this place is like the Swamp of Sadness in *The Neverending Story* and my car's gonna get swallowed up like Atreyu's horse. I press my foot down on the pedal. The tires spin and the car slides a little bit from side to side, but I'm definitely stuck. Like, it's not even worth me trying to get out level of stuck.

This could not be worse.

With an exasperated growl, I open the car door. I can only open it about a foot, because I'm so deep in the mud that the door hits a rock. Great. Using my best athletic abilities, I wriggle out and launch myself to the side of the path. I almost fall backward into the mud, but at the last second I catch hold of a tree branch and steady myself. It's not graceful, but it works.

So I guess not *everything* about nature is bad. I give the tree a little pat of thanks and start on an unsteady trek the rest of the way to the stupid Haven. It's not far but it's not a fun walk. I'm staying to the edge of the road so that my shoes don't get coated in mud, but the ground still oozes even here on the edges, and my sneakers are looking a bit browner than they did when I left school. I haven't seen any ticks yet, and fall isn't their most active season, but I still can't stop feeling like one's crawling on me.

I'm not even going to think about the larger dangers that might be out here. Bears, wolves. Not much I can do if one of those finds me.

I haven't been walking long when I notice what looks like a footpath branching off from this main road. It's extremely narrow, and if it weren't fall, I don't think I'd even have noticed it through the leaves. I wonder if, by chance, it circumvents this monstrosity of a mud pit they call a road. If it starts to lead me too far astray, I can always turn back, but for now, I decide to risk it.

The ground is much drier on this path. I made the right choice. Wispy tree branches grab hold of my arms as I pass by, but other than that, not too much obstructs me. Once away from the road, the path widens a tiny bit. Enough so that the branches aren't in my way anymore. I'm heading away from the road, but curiosity has gotten the better of me, so I'm going to follow the path and see if it meets back up somewhere.

It doesn't.

It ends after I've been walking for about another ten minutes. And it ends at a small concrete building backed up against a steep, rocky hill. To call it a building is maybe too strong. It's outhouse-sized, maybe five feet square. It's taller than me, but only by a few inches, and the roof is a flat concrete slab. What is this building and what's it doing out here away from the commune? Part of me doesn't want to know, but a much larger part of me knows that I am absolutely going to open that door.

It's heavy. The door isn't concrete like the rest; it's made of thick metal, and it is quite narrow. But the hinges are a little rusty, and the door's thicker than a normal one, so I have to use both hands to swing it wide.

Inside, there's . . . nothing. It's a windowless, concrete box. I hold up my phone's flashlight to see if I'm missing something hidden away in one of its darker corners, but it's empty. The floor has a couple of vaguely rust-colored streaks that unsettle me a little, but upon closer inspection, I don't think they're blood. I'm telling myself they're not, anyway.

The inside of the door doesn't have a handle. The outside of the door has a lock.

I don't know why this building is here or what it's used for, but whatever its purpose, it isn't good. If you got trapped in there and the lock was closed . . . I don't know if anyone could even hear you scream. I push the door closed, the way I found it, and that's when I notice the tiny circled logo engraved in the metal. The *H* is distinct, the word *verum* barely legible.

So this belongs to the Haven, too. Awesome.

I back away, quickly, and trot back the way I came until I meet the road. This place is the worst. I'm getting Cara out of here the moment she's willing to come, and we are never looking back.

Finally, after what feels like a century of walking, I make it to the field that edges the commune. Cara's car is parked here. It's dirt-streaked, too; looks like whenever she last drove it, she didn't have an easy time, either. I spot her immediately. She's standing by the fire pit, talking to a couple other girls. Jealousy flares in my chest. She looks happy, animated. Avalon clings to her leg.

Are these new friends better than me? I don't understand why. They're nothing like anyone we hang out with at home. They're nothing like Cara and me. At least, the Cara I thought I knew.

My eyes lower to Avalon. I suspect that little girl is a big part of the draw, and I want to be happy for Cara to have found someone who can patch up the hole in her heart, but I'm not. All I feel is resentment. Mixed with some guilt and shame over my selfishness.

Cara hasn't noticed me yet. I remind myself that there's a pretty big expanse of space between us, but right now it feels like the expanse is more than physical. I lean my shoulder against a pine that towers behind her car. I'm a little chilly and I realize it was moronic to wear only a sweatshirt and not consider that it'd be cooler in the dappled light of the forest, shaded by the towering pines.

I'm being creepy, I guess, standing here watching my best friend talk to other people. But I'm just trying to decide if she looks like that when she talks to me. I think she does. Or used to.

I sweep my eyes across the Haven, looking for familiar faces. I should have interacted with more people when I came before. I remember hardly anyone's names, and that's going to make me look like a real jerk.

One of the girls with Cara spots me, and points. Cara gestures me over, an exaggerated leaping wave of both hands, and I can't help the grin that spreads over my face. I disentangle from the tree and trot over, not caring how dumb and over-eager I look.

Cara hugs me when I reach her; it feels familiar and normal and I don't want to let go.

"You came!" Cara says. She squeezes my hand and then pulls away.

"Of course I came. Can't let you celebrate the harvest all by yourself, can I?"

Avalon giggles, and I'm not sure why. I glance down at her with a hesitant smile. She hides her face in Cara's side. The behavior seems a little young, but I guess six-year-olds can be shy sometimes, too.

"Been a while since we've seen you," says one of the other girls.

"Yeah." I try to smile again, but it goes even worse than before. "I mean, I have school and drama club and everything, and I know you guys have a pretty scheduled routine."

"Can I talk to you alone for a minute, Mailee?" Cara intercedes.

Gladly.

I extricate myself from the other two and I'm trying not to look smug but my face is doing it anyway. Cara walks me back toward the spot where her car is parked; away from the camp itself. She looks around confusedly.

"Where'd you park?" she asks.

"Oh, just in the middle of the mud puddle where I got stuck."

"Ugh, I'm sorry, Mailee. I should've warned you that the road up was pretty bad. Firehorse should be able to pull you out."

"Thanks. I hope he can. It's *really* stuck." I consider telling her about the weird concrete structure I found, but she's being so friendly, I don't want her to get defensive.

"I really wanted you to come tonight," Cara says. "I'm glad you did."

"Me too." I lock down the sense of foreboding her expression gives me.

"So I misled you a tiny bit about what this celebration is for." She brushes a streak of dust off the hood of her car, not meeting my eye. "I wasn't sure if you'd come if I told you everything."

My stomach turns to lava. "It's not a harvest celebration?"

"No, it is. I mean, it's that and also . . . it's going to feature my initiation ceremony," she says hastily. "I'm going to become a member of the Haven. I'm going to live here."

"You're . . . *what*?" I have to keep calm. The worst thing I can do right now is to lose it about this but I am reeling. Totally blindsided. "Look, Cara, I know you like hanging out here, but your parents are never going to let you do this."

"You know when my birthday is," she says coolly.

Next week. She'll be eighteen. "I see."

The expression on her face shifts; her brows pull together and her lips twitch down. "I really want you to stay. It would mean so much to me if you were here for this and if . . . well, I think Firehorse would let you join, too. We could both live here!"

Why would I *ever* want to? Has she totally forgotten who I am? Who *she* is? That's what I want to say, but I restrain myself. "I'll stay tonight," I decide. "But joining . . . I'm not exactly a living-in-the-woods kind of girl. You know that."

"I didn't think I was, either, but it's not so bad. If I can do it, you can do it. And it's really . . ." Something in her expression darkens again. There are secrets behind her eyes. "It's safe here. I want you to be safe here with me."

"Safe from what?"

"Come on." She grabs my arm and pulls me back toward the camp. "I'll let Firehorse explain the rest about the ceremony."

If she wasn't tugging on me, I'm not sure my feet would have lifted on their own. I came expecting a party, maybe kind of a weird party, but not this. Not secrets and not my best friend leaving me forever to live like a modern caveperson. How am I supposed to become a famous actress if I live in the woods forever? Suddenly, I wish I'd said yes when Gavin asked if he should come. I thought having him here would be too raw; Cara hasn't wanted to be around the two of us together ever since what happened with Jackson, and I don't want to push her away even more. But she's pushing *herself* away. At least Gavin could help me figure out what to do next.

Cara knocks on the door of Firehorse's shack. One thing I'll give him is that his shack is no fancier than any of the others. He's their leader, but his living accommodations and his food intake are no different than anyone else's, and that's respectable. Still, I have developed such a visceral dislike of him. When he comes swaggering out with his shoulder-length gray-peppered brown hair and his demonically blue eyes, I suppress a shudder. I don't know how I was so drawn in by him at first.

Everything about him screams fake. Right now he's walking slowly, whittling something with his giant hunting knife. But I'm skeptical that he even knows what he's doing. It all seems like a big show. At least he's not wearing his dumb dream-catcher necklace today.

I didn't realize, until now, that all my hurt at Cara's abandonment was covering up another feeling, a sense of concern. There's something not right about this place. About Firehorse. This hippie toxin-free vegan commune front is hiding something about Firehorse's true goals. If only I knew *what*, though.

"Greetings, Mailee," Firehorse says. He puts away his whittling project and hooks his thumbs on either side of his belt buckle, which is a new, unique touch to his appearance. The buckle is white, sort of odd shaped, maybe a stone.

I suppress an eye roll. "Greetings."

"I'm glad to see you here." He doesn't sound glad at all. But I can't bring myself to say I'm happy to be here, so I guess we're even. He lets the awkward silence stretch on between us, probably trying to get me to say something. I stay strong, even though I can feel Cara radiating unhappiness from beside me. If Firehorse doesn't care if I'm comfortable, then I don't care if he is, either.

The rest of the commune is slowly and quietly encircling us. Like a cohort of ants that's found a big dying bug; reaching out eagerly to start tearing into its flesh before its life has even ended.

Firehorse claps his hands together delightedly. "Let's get started, then."

I turn around. The metal side of his shack is icy against my shoulder blades, even through my sweatshirt. But from here, I can see everyone semicircled around us, and I feel slightly less uncomfortable.

"We are delighted," Firehorse begins, "to finally initiate Cara as one of our own. She has been working very hard toward this for months, and I'm so happy, as I'm sure we all are, to see her work pay off."

The gathered semicircle claps enthusiastically. Cara's grin is monstrous. She isn't looking at me at all, but Firehorse is, out of the corner of his eye. Reluctantly, I join in the clapping, feeling very much like an outsider.

"Our mission is an important one," Firehorse continues, and he cracks a knowing smile at the group. "Not that any of you need reminding."

His eyes flick to me again, and my discomfort grows.

"This initiation ceremony is going to be *extra* special. It'll be our last, and we'll be visiting the Cave for the end of the ritual. I'm very excited that the first harvest celebration will be such a memorable event."

Something about the way he says *cave* feels like it's asking for capitalization and I'm not so sure how I feel about that. I don't like the way he says the word *harvest*, either, like he's got an inside joke going with himself. I hold in my questions, though. Stay quiet, Mailee. Now's the time to just go along with things. Getting Cara out of this will have to come when we're not surrounded.

And when she doesn't look so . . .

Adoring.

The way she's looking at Firehorse, I want to be sick. It's the way you look at a parent, or the way I used to look at my older brother when we were kids and I thought he knew everything. What has he done to deserve that look from her? He's no one.

"Your trust, your belief, it's more important now than ever. When the world changes, when everything falls apart and people are desperate, it will make all the difference. You will be safe. *We* will be safe. We have all made sacrifices, and we have been very patient. But it's near now, I can feel it. Can you all feel it?"

Everyone nods. Even Cara. I'm frozen. I know Firehorse is watching me again but I don't know what the hell is going on here, what I'm supposed to feel or trust or *believe*. I can't make myself nod.

"Good," Firehorse says, almost to himself. Then, more loudly, "Let's prepare, then. It's a long trip out to the Cave."

The group disperses, and they all start shouldering hiking backpacks. Wait. We're going somewhere else, somewhere . . . out in the woods? And we're going *right now*.

I mentally rewind through everything Firehorse just said, and my stomach seizes with a sudden realization. Something I should've seen much, much sooner.

This place is *not* a hippie commune.

It's a cult.

SIXTEEN

"Cara. You need to tell me what's going on. *Now.*"

She and I are alone in one of the metal shacks, but I don't think we have long. I need to get her to leave this place, which means I need to be nicer but I am so freaked out and *so* furious.

"It's a harvest celebration, like I told you before. And my initiation ceremony is the highlight." She hauls on a hiking backpack the size of her body. "I don't know all the details about it, because you're not supposed to know beforehand. I just know that we have to go to the Cave, and that the whole event lasts three days with, like, traveling and stuff."

"*Three days?* Cara, I told Gavin I'd be back tomorrow. He's going to freak out. Not to mention my parents, who don't even know where I am. If I don't go home or even call for three freaking days, I will be grounded until I'm out of college."

"Don't worry about that. Firehorse has a phone with one of those range extender things on it. He'll let you call them on the way. Just tell your parents we're on a weekend camping trip. They won't care."

Gavin will, though. He'll know something's wrong. And something is definitely wrong here. "I thought Firehorse was against cell phones. Because of the electromagnetic field thing."

She glares. "He is. That's why everyone has necklaces or bracelets, even up here." She gestures to the dumb necklace she's been wearing since the summer. "He keeps a cell phone for just in case, and a laptop, too."

"Are you sure he'll let me use his phone?"

"Of course! Why wouldn't you think so?"

"I don't know. I don't think he likes me that much."

"That's ridiculous. Of course he likes you. You know how you read too much into things."

The door screeches open and I jump. It's Firehorse, no surprise. I give him my realest fake smile, but inside I'm quaking. I don't feel jittery like this very often, and I store the feeling—and my reactions—away to write down later in my emotions journal.

"We were just talking about you," Cara says. She's completely at ease, not worried about angering Firehorse at all. I've never seen him actually act on feelings of anger, so I don't know why I'm worried about it, either. Something about this ceremony just makes me feel so wrong inside, I regret coming. What else would I have done, though? Cara's parents clearly think this place is fine or they'd be doing much more to keep her from visiting. Nonstop. And I don't have any evidence otherwise, besides this soul-deep bad feeling.

"Were you? Only good things, I hope," Firehorse teases with a chuckle that crawls up my spine.

There's nothing wrong about the way he says it. He's not sleazy, isn't standing too close or acting differently than any other man his age should. Am I reading too much into this situation, like Cara said? Should I be giving him more credit? He's not forcing Cara to be here. She's made this crazy choice on her own, no question. It's not against the law to run a commune—or a cult—as long as you're not hurting anyone. I will myself to calm down. Until he gives me a reason not to, I need to give Firehorse the benefit of the doubt. For Cara. For getting her back home where she belongs.

"Yeah, I was just telling Cara that I didn't realize I'd be gone the whole weekend. I need to tell my parents and I don't have cell service. She told me I'd be able to use yours?"

My eyes flick to his wrist, and Cara wasn't wrong. He's wearing a bracelet. Presumably with the same nonsense technology that's in her necklace.

"Yes, of course!" Firehorse pats me kindly on the shoulder. I'm not repulsed. *Not* repulsed. "Yes, once we get on our way. It gets better service a little deeper in the woods, funnily enough."

That's not suspicious at all. Totally logical.

"Okay. Thank you. Also . . . not to be high maintenance, but my car got stuck on the way here."

Firehorse's pleasant smile falters for a moment. "How far back?"

Far enough to see that concrete cell you've got out there. "I think I was walking for a little less than a half hour."

"Ah, yes, the road does get quite muddy back there. Unfortunately, I won't have time to pull you out before we go on our trek, but I certainly will when we get back. We aren't supposed to get rain this weekend, so hopefully the mud will have dried up some by then, anyway. That'll help."

"Okay. That works." Although, honestly, I'd rather just have my car back and get the heck out of here.

"I came to bring you this." Firehorse holds up a necklace nearly identical to Cara's. Oh great.

"I'm all set, thank you."

He pushes the necklace toward me. "While you're here, I'm going to ask that you wear it. After a couple days, I really think you'll notice a difference in your energy and mental clarity."

"Sure, okay." It comes out a little sarcastic despite my best efforts. When I put on the necklace, nothing feels different. Big surprise.

"Listen." Firehorse's voice is serious now. "Mailee, Cara's told me you're not much of an outdoors person."

"Yeah . . . that's an understatement."

He chuckles. "Well, don't you worry. We'll take care of you out there. Many of our members knew nothing about nature before they came here. There was once a time when even I knew only the easy pleasures of city life. But we all help each other and work together and the outdoors, the simpler life, none of it is so hard."

"Will there be a lot of spiders during the hike?" I ask in my tiniest voice.

Neither laughs meanly, but they do both laugh. My face burns.

"There will most likely be some spiders," Firehorse says. "But probably not big ones."

That is *not* comforting.

"What about other animals? Like bears and stuff?"

"They're around. But you'll be perfectly safe with the group. Just don't wander off." He smiles broadly, like that's an amusing and not at all threatening joke. "And since you haven't done much hiking, we won't make you wear a full-sized backpack," he adds, and holds up a backpack not much larger— though quite a bit more stuffed—than my school backpack. "This will suffice. The rest of us will be happy to share our supplies with you."

"Oh. Thank you." His ostensibly kind gesture makes me feel like a giant burden, which irritates me since I wasn't even warned that I would be going on a hike at all, let alone a multi-day hike.

"It's getting dark soon," Firehorse says, "So we'll need to get on our way if we want to get in much hiking this evening. Mailee, do you believe in us?"

His abrupt question catches me off guard. What does he even mean? "Um . . . yes?"

He tilts his head to one side, the tightness of his eyes telling me that won't cut it.

"Yes. Of course."

A satisfied nod tells me I did okay this time.

Cara and I follow him out of the metal shack, letting the door fall closed behind us with a banshee-shriek of rusted metal on metal. Once we're slightly away from him, mixed in with the group, I turn to her.

"So just to clarify, all we know about this is that there's some kind of ceremony at a cave, and that we're going to be gone three days?"

"We also know that we'll probably get to the Cave mid-afternoon tomorrow."

"Do we know anything about the cave?"

"Not really," Cara says. "There's a lot of stuff you just don't get to know until you are an official commune member, which is understandable. But they all talk very seriously about the Cave, so I know it's a big deal."

"If there's stuff you're not supposed to know unless you're official, what happens if I witness the whole ceremony and then I decide not to join?" Because I am definitely not joining.

"Firehorse said it wouldn't be a problem." But for the first time, I detect a hint of concern in her voice.

"Okay. But, Cara, doesn't it bother you, not knowing anything about this? Being left totally in the dark? Usually, you're organized down to the minute."

"And where has that gotten me, huh?" Her voice darkens. "It's gotten me nowhere. The Haven has been teaching me how to let things go. How to be part of something worth believing in. How to let someone *else* do the organizing and the planning, and just follow the schedule."

"But you—"

"All right, everyone!" Firehorse's cheerful voice cuts me off. "Time to go!"

I guess I'm doing this. I guess I'm going hiking and sleeping in a tent and praying to God a spider doesn't build a web around me during the night. Or that I don't get sprayed in the face by a skunk. Or eaten by a grizzly bear.

The path we're taking is narrow and steep; it looks more like a dusty rut that a long-dried stream left in the hill than an actual path. I slip a lot on the way up, banging my hands and knees on sharp-edged rocks.

By the time we reach the top, sweat pours from me and I'm panting like I've just finished a two-hundred-meter sprint. I don't want to say anything about how much I'm struggling because my backpack is, like, a quarter the size of everyone else's, but wow does this not bode well for the rest of the trip.

I pull my cell phone out of my back pocket and after one last longing glance at its screen, I shut it off. No point in wasting the battery. I won't even begin to have reception out here. I pull the backpack around to my front to stow the phone with my keys in the small pocket.

Except.

My keys aren't there.

"Hey, um, Firehorse?" I start nervously. "I think my keys fell out on the way up the path. You didn't happen to see them fall, did you?"

"Don't you think I'd have let you know?"

Oh. I guess.

"Right. Sorry. Will I be able to catch up? I really need to go back and look for them."

"I'm sure you just put them in the wrong pocket, Mailee. We've got to keep on, but I promise when you're ready to leave, if you haven't found the keys, we'll all help."

He still sounds so nice and so helpful, but my alarm bells are going off like crazy. He has my keys, I know it. There's not a shred of doubt in my mind.

"Okay," I say meekly. "Thank you."

Firehorse has stolen my car keys. And even *with* my keys, my car is hopelessly stuck. Cara doesn't know—and is clearly at least a *touch* worried—what will happen if I don't join the commune after witnessing the event at the Cave. It's too much. My remaining fraying threads of chill snap, and in a panic, I find Cara and pull her slightly off to the side. We're probably still within earshot of others, but I'm desperate.

"Cara, please, I'm begging you. Can we not do this? I am so uncomfortable, and I think Firehorse has my keys, and we don't know what's going to happen at that cave and it's just—"

"*Mailee.*" She cuts off my words, wielding my name like a fist that cracks me across the cheek. "For once, could you just support me at something? Everything is not about what you want. Can you just be here for *me* this *one time*?"

Every word is another fist; my emotions are seeping blood by the time she's finished those three tiny sentences. Why can't she see that this situation isn't good? Why can't she see that underneath the kindness and the cowboy boots, Firehorse is hiding something? My throat is thick with hurt, and before I can formulate a response, a shadow falls over me.

I know who it is without turning around.

"Mailee, it sounds like we need to have a little talk, just you and I," Firehorse says.

Cara is smiling adoringly at him as he leads me away. I squeeze and unsqueeze my hands to try to hide the fact that I'm shaking like a fall leaf about to be severed from its tree by the wind.

Firehorse stands very close to me this time. His gaze pierces me.

"It is important to Cara that you be here." His voice is even, but a quiver of anger runs beneath, and it tears at my resolve. "And because of that, you are necessary to this celebration, whether you join us or not. And this celebration, Cara's joining, is necessary for our group. The *most* necessary. It completes us."

Why, though? Every statement he just made needs more explanation. I am literally biting my tongue to stop myself from speaking.

"I thought that we had an understanding, Mailee, after our conversation during your last visit. I know it's been a while, but I thought we were friends."

"We are." I can barely pry the words from my throat.

"Good." He places a hand on my shoulder in what probably looks like a kind gesture from afar, but his fingers are squeezing and it hurts.

I say nothing.

"But if we are to be friends, Mailee, you need to trust me. And I need to trust you. And if you don't think you can do that, we will have a very serious problem."

My eyes flicker to the knife at his belt. He's not touching it, his hands are nowhere near it, in fact. But I feel like somehow, he's reminding me it's there. For a moment, I consider running. He might not come after me if I barreled back down the hill and just *fled*. But where would I go? I have no keys, my car is stuck in the mud, and I would be running a *long* time before I could find reception and what if he *did* come after me? Then I'd be in real trouble.

No, the only way to get myself—and Cara—out of this is to play along.

For now.

I give him my movie-star smile one more time. "We won't have a problem. I promise. I'm sorry, I know you didn't take my keys, I just . . . I don't really like camping and I got freaked out."

"That is perfectly understandable. And I know I can trust that it will be the last time we hear such an outburst from you." He returns my expression with a pretty stellar movie-star smile of his own. He gives my shoulder one last sharp squeeze, and then he lets me go, thumbs hooking on either side of his belt buckle as he turns away, back toward the group.

And that's when I realize with a sharp jolt of discomfort what the belt buckle is actually made of. It's a bone. A vertebra.

I don't like this at all. But I'm here, and Cara's here. We're stuck.

For now.

SEVENTEEN

Cara regrets inviting me now. My fit of panic basically ruined everything, and I'm scared I won't be able to fix it. I'm doing everything I can, but she's frozen harder than a shallow lake in the dead of winter.

As is everyone else in the group. I'm not a queen bee or anything at school, but I'm not a pariah, either, and I don't know how to handle it. As dusk starts spreading shadows over the forest floor, Firehorse "remembers" that I need to use his range extender, but mysteriously, he just cannot manage to get service. He seems to think his faux surprised expression is really great, but it's not fooling me for a second.

"I'm *always* able to get service out here," he says with a tiny pout. "I'm so sorry, Mailee. We'll try again in the morning, when we're a bit farther in."

I pull out my fake smile again. "Absolutely. Maybe it's too cloudy. Tomorrow will be better."

We both know it's not too cloudy. And so does Cara, who

stands nearby, looking like she can't decide whether to involve herself.

"I like your positive attitude, Mailee," is all Firehorse replies. Then he claps his hands together and turns to the group. "Time to set up camp, everyone! This is where we'll stay for the night."

Cara approaches me. "We're sharing a tent," she says in a detached voice. "You don't have to help me set it up, though."

"No, I want to help. Just tell me what to do."

She arches an eyebrow. "Really?"

"Look, Cara, I'm here. I'm camping. If I'm going to be part of it, I want to be part of it. Camping is a good life experience, right? I'll never be a real actress if I don't have life experiences."

A frown tugs briefly at the corners of her mouth, but she recovers quickly. "All right, then. Let's get to work."

It turns out, I'm actually awesome at putting up a tent. Yes, this was a two-person tent specifically styled to be easily put together, but that's beside the point. I rocked it.

"Look at this!" I exclaim, crawling inside and flopping down on top of my sleeping bag. I poke at the edge of the tent. "We put together a tent and it doesn't collapse when touched!"

Cara rolls out her sleeping bag beside mine. "Not collapsing to the touch is kind of the goal, you know."

"I know, but *we* did it. Would you have thought?"

She smiles at my genuine enthusiasm. "I guess I wouldn't have."

I wait for her to say more—to turn the moment dark by making it about the commune. *See? Look how the Haven has made us more awesome!* But, to my relief, she doesn't say a word.

I guess she didn't have to.

"I know today didn't get off to the best start," I tell her, "but I'm really happy you asked me to come. I've missed you. A lot."

She reaches for my hand and squeezes. "I've missed you, too."

Pressure wells up behind my eyes, and I blink hard to stop the tears before they come. Cara doesn't need to know right now how much it's hurt not to have her around. She's obviously been hurting, too. Worse. That's why it's been like this. I need to be the strong one, I need to be her rock.

A face pokes into our tent and I nearly jump out of my skin. It's Finn. "Hey, look who successfully put up a tent!" he says, not mean-spiritedly.

"That's right, we did!" Cara says proudly. "And our tent is *way* better than your tent."

"Well, there's girls in it, so yeah, I'd say so." He grins at her.

I get a pit in my stomach. They're flirting again, or still, or whatever. That's . . . not going to make this easier. Maybe if I can get him to flirt with *me* so she feels betrayed . . . no, I don't want to do that to her. Not to mention that the plan hinges on Finn being a gross jerk and I haven't had enough interactions with him to assume that's the case. All I know is, he scowls a lot.

He reaches out a hand to Cara and pulls her up, out of the tent. "Fire's started and everyone's eating," he says.

I crawl clumsily out of the tent, trailing behind them like a third wheel. No wonder Cara didn't like hanging out with Gavin and me after her breakup. This is beyond awkward. *Don't worry guys! I didn't need help up or anything!* I'm pretty proud of myself for keeping my snarky little thoughts in my head.

Dinner is some kind of bean soup and asparagus. The asparagus is good, roasted over the fire, but we had to cook so much of it to feed everyone. It feels unsustainable. It also most definitely did not come from the small garden they've got planted by the commune.

Brigit sits beside me. I'm surprised. Last time we talked, I felt like, I don't know. Like maybe I stressed her out. Or got her in trouble.

"Hi, Mailee," she says. "It's been a while."

"It has, I know. I've been so busy with school, and drama club. I'm glad Cara invited me to this, though." If I say it enough times in that enthusiastic voice, maybe I'll start to believe it.

"I'm excited to finally see the Cave," Brigit says.

"You've never seen it? I thought that was, like, where initiation ceremonies happened?"

"Oh, no. No, the rest of us were initiated right at the Haven. Cara's special because we won't be accepting more members after her. There's only so many resources if you don't want to eat meat, you know?"

"Yeah, true. Cara's really excited about it. I'm glad to see her so happy about something." I am becoming an excellent liar.

"Cara is really great," Brigit says, but her voice lacks conviction. Part of me wants to wax poetic about all the ways Cara *is* great, but part of me wonders . . . what makes Brigit not like her?

I notice that she's eaten everything on her plate except the bottom couple inches of all her stalks of asparagus. "Saving the best part for last?" I ask, pointing my fork at her plate.

She chuckles. "Listen. Just because I'm vegan doesn't mean I have to like all the vegetables out there. I can eat asparagus if I have to, but I cannot make myself choke down the thick part of the stem. It's gross."

"I feel the same way about broccoli. Tops only."

"Good luck. I'm pretty sure broccoli's on the menu for tomorrow night." She tosses one of her asparagus ends into the fire, where it sizzles and shrivels. "Don't do what I just did, by the way. Firehorse hates it when we waste food."

I glance up to where Firehorse is sitting with Alexa, Cara, and Finn on the other side of the fire. He's too engaged in conversation to notice what Brigit is doing. She's a little rebellious, and I like it.

"Can I try?" I ask.

She grins and holds out her plate. One of the other girls frowns disapprovingly as the asparagus chunk hits the flames, but Firehorse didn't see.

"It's fun, isn't it?" Brigit says. She gathers the rest of her asparagus into her fist and tosses them behind us, into the trees. "I don't like to push it, though."

"What . . . would happen if you did?" I ask.

"I don't know." She runs a hand over her arm, like suddenly she's chilled. "But Firehorse doesn't really like to be tested."

I look through the wavering flames at Firehorse again. Smiling, laughing, totally at ease. But I've seen darkness in his eyes, I've felt it in his tone of voice. I think about my earlier revelation, about this being a cult, not a commune. It's not like today was the very first time it crossed my mind, but I dismissed it before. Now I don't know how I ever did.

Last week, Samantha sent me a link to an article on cults and how they recruit. Deception, manipulation, isolation. All I texted back was, LOL. But the signs are there. Firehorse is crazy manipulative. He cut Cara off from me, and as much as everyone's pretending it's fine that I'm here, it's obvious to me that I was not part of the plan. Cara got a wild hair and now they have to pretend to be fine with it to save face. Control, that was another thing. And there's this underlying current of fear no one's really open about. Firehorse has created a routine for these people and when they don't follow it, he is *mad*.

I'm starting to get kind of angry, thinking about it. Who is Firehorse, even? He's no one. He might have gotten these others, but he will *not* have Cara.

Tents are creepy. Even sharing the space with Cara doesn't help. Shadows from tree limbs overhead weave patterns over the thin fabric. Only the shadows don't look like tree limbs, they look like claws outstretched, and then closing into fists when the wind shifts. Or the lithe bodies of murderers, edging closer, waiting for me to fall asleep.

I'm edgy, and I flick on the flashlight from Cara's pack for about the sixth time since we got settled into bed.

"Mailee," Cara groans. "You are driving me crazy with that thing."

"Sorry." I aim it toward the corner of the tent and am about to shut it off when I see movement. My heart stops. It's my worst-case scenario (besides a murderer).

A spider is in here.

I have one of those moments, like a woman who heroically finds the physical strength to lift a car off her child, and I whip the butt of the flashlight forward and slam it down on top of the spider, grinding hard. My whole body thrums with adrenaline as I lift the flashlight. Little bits of spider flesh dangle from the end. A severed leg falls, and I suppress a scream.

"What are you *doing* over there?" Cara grumbles.

"Nothing." I turn off the flashlight and burrow into my sleeping bag. "Good night."

She mutters something incoherent that I think is also a "good night" and her breathing deepens almost immediately. What I wouldn't give to be able to sleep as easily as she does.

I am trying really hard to be brave but the spider was too much for me. Could there be others? Could one be crawling on me right now? I press my face into my pillow and let tears come, as quietly as I can manage. As much as I hate spiders, I've never cried over one before, and Cara won't understand.

Because it's not about the spider, it's about all of this. She misled me on purpose to get me out here, and now I'm stuck and I just want to call my parents and ask them to please, please come get me—come get both of us—but that would require cell service, of which there is none. I keep having these bursts of resolve where I feel like I want to take down Firehorse single-handedly, like I'm going to tap into this previously unknown source of power within myself and shoot laser beams out of my eyes that fry him to dust. But alone in the dark with the shadows and the spider and the isolation, that resolve melts away, replaced with unadulterated terror.

When Samantha sent me that article about cults, I laughed it off. Like, yeah, the Haven is a strange place, and there were maybe some red flags, but you read about cults in thinkpieces online; you don't run into them in real life. I should have seen all the signs, and I should *never* have come up here alone without cell service, leaving my car stuck in mud and totally unusable. I am not this dumb. It's just . . . part of me never believed anything bad would happen. And still refuses to believe it.

The other part is completely and utterly lost trying to understand how to get out of this. Especially since Cara is so drawn in, it's not even funny.

"Hey, Cara," I whisper, poking her until she rolls over toward me and opens her eyes. "What did Firehorse say that convinced you to live at the Haven? Like, what was *the* thing that cemented it for you?"

She sighs and rubs her eyes. "It wasn't Firehorse who convinced me. It was Avalon."

Great.

"She told me Firehorse was so pleased that Alexa had brought me into the group. That Alexa was so pleased, too. Everyone, and most of all, herself. I don't know. She's a sweet kid, Mailee, and she needs me. Everyone's happy to have me here. No judgment, no . . . it's just nice. I fit. I feel unburdened."

Why you, *though?* I want to ask. But there's no way to ask without sounding insulting. Cara's great. Beyond great. But the fact that they were all *so* pleased, specifically about her, after meeting her once . . . I don't know. It sketches me out big time.

The question I ask her instead isn't much better: "Was I . . . making you feel burdened?"

She blinks at me. "Good night, Mailee. I'm too tired to talk anymore."

"Good night," I whisper, and turn back to face the side of the tent and the bits of squished spider. I am that spider now. And Cara just ground the butt of that flashlight into my heart.

EIGHTEEN

I think it goes without saying that I slept like crap. On the plus side, no other spiders infiltrated our tent after the first one. At least, none that I saw. For breakfast, we had granola. No yogurt, of course. But the granola obviously came from a store—"Firehorse still buys some stuff while we work to become fully self-sustaining," is how Cara explained it—and if you're going to a store anyway, there must at *least* be some kind of dairy-free yogurt alternative.

But I'm trying not to complain, and I'm trying to appear like I'm falling into the folds of this whole thing. I even smile kindly at Finn, a piece of acting that I personally feel should win me an Oscar. It's easier to smile at Alexa, who comes to help when we struggle a bit with the whole taking-down-our-tent business.

"It's one of those things where they make it so easy it becomes hard," she says. I can't tell if this is supposed to be nice or mean. "If you do it the exact way it's meant to be done, you can fold it up in two seconds, but if you deviate even a tiny bit, it takes forever. You'll get it with practice."

I glance across the clearing to where Alexa's tent was set up last night. "Is that Avalon taking down your tent?"

"Yep."

"Well *that's* not embarrassing at all," says Cara.

Alexa laughs. "Would it help if I remind you that little kids learn new skills way faster? And that Avalon's been doing this a whole lot longer than you anyway?"

"I'm going to pretend that makes me feel like less of a failure," I say, and Cara and I both watch Alexa as she shows us how to fold the poles from our tent.

She wasn't wrong. It's super easy if you do it the right way. Which, clearly, we didn't.

"Now I'd better go help Avalon. She does fine taking the tent apart, but not so much attaching it to the pack."

Alexa trots off, and I watch her go. She and Avalon both seem so happy and content here. Watching them, it's hard to believe anything malicious might be going on. But then I catch a glimpse of Brigit eyeing Firehorse nervously, and I wonder how much information Alexa just doesn't have. Same as me, minus the skepticism.

Finn sweeps Cara away as we start walking, and I feel like a major outcast. I edge toward Brigit, the only person I feel like I've formed any kind of bond with at all, but just as I reach her, Firehorse swoops between us.

"What's your parents' number?" he asks.

"Why?"

"I'm still not getting cell service even with my range extender," he says. "So I'm going to try climbing a tree to contact them."

This feels super made up, but it's not like I can demand to join him in the tree. Even if he said yes, I can't even begin to climb one.

If I get out of this alive, I'm taking a wilderness survival course ASAP.

I type my parents' number into his phone, all the while feeling Brigit's eyes boring into my back.

"Please let me know what they say," I tell him. "And tell them I'm really sorry the trip is longer than I expected, but Cara and I are having fun."

He beams at me. I do my best to match the expression, then watch as he does, indeed, scale a tree and dial his phone.

"What are the odds he's actually talking to my parents?" I say to Brigit.

She raises both eyebrows. Right. She can say subtle things, but apparently it's not cool if I openly question whether Firehorse is a liar.

"Don't mind me." I kick at a rock with my toe and send it skittering off the path. "I didn't sleep that great, and I'm a little cranky."

"I understand," she says. And then after a brief silence, adds, "You seem to be good at reading people, though."

She probably has no idea what a compliment that is to me, but I'm so pleased that I feel myself starting to blush. "I want to be an actress one day. So it's important to really understand body language and facial cues and stuff."

"Huh. I would never have thought about that." Brigit stuffs her hands into the pockets of her jeans. "Anyway, I just . . . wouldn't let yourself get talked out of trusting your gut, is all."

"I—"

"Hey, Mailee!" I glance behind me, following the sound of my name. It's Richelle, one of the girls who Cara seems to have particularly bonded with. I feel like I'm not a fan, but "because Cara likes her too much and I'm jealous" is probably a pretty bad reason not to like someone. "Cara wants you to come walk with us!"

I glance at Brigit, fully intending to bring her with me, but she waves me off. "I'll talk to you later," she says.

And as I walk away, I swear I hear her add: "It's probably for the best."

A chill runs down my spine.

Cara's *very* chipper, skipping along with her group of friends like this is a school field trip or something. I have to remind myself that we're the only high schoolers here. The others may be young, but they're not as young as us. Including Finn, who she's starting to look a little more than platonic with. Guess I don't blame her. But it doesn't mean I trust him. Or any of them.

Or even Cara, right now.

Which is a thought that makes me very, very sad.

"Oh my God, Mailee," she says, voice filled with laughter when she spots me. "You have to hear this story Finn was just telling about the first time he went camping with the group. It is *hilarious*."

To be honest, I am not interested in this story at all, but for her sake, I pretend. Finn weaves a pretty good tale, I can't lie. I am actually laughing a real laugh by the end, listening to him talk about tent collapse, tick overreactions, and tripping and rolling down a steep hill like a boulder.

"So you and Mailee really aren't doing all that bad for your first time," he says, slipping an arm around Cara's waist. I glare at his hand, and Richelle catches me. I quickly rearrange my face.

"Good to know," I say. "Because I'm a pretty serious camping virgin."

"Yeah, her parents took her and her brother to a campground once in—what was it, Mailee, like, fourth grade? And she had so little tolerance for it that they had to leave in the middle of the night and never tried it again."

They laugh, but it doesn't feel like the same as when everyone laughed at Finn's story. It's the hurtful kind of laughter, where everyone acts like they're laughing with you, but really they're laughing at how much they think you suck.

"What can I say?" I keep my voice light. "I've always been an indoors girl."

"But outside is *so fun*," says Avalon. Great, I'm getting put down by a six-year-old.

"Outside has a lot of spiders," I tell her.

That's when Alexa joins us, emerging from the trees at the side of the path. She smirks, but Avalon just looks befuddled. "Spiders can't hurt you, Mailee."

Maybe not the ones we have around here, but has she heard of black widows? Or the freaking brown recluse? Or the Brazilian wandering spider? Alexa throws me a look that says *do not pass along your irrational fear to my child*, so I keep my mouth shut about it.

"I know they can't. I just don't like how many legs they have."

"I wish *I* had eight legs." Avalon sighs wistfully. "I could run so fast."

"Yeah?" I laugh. Some of the people here creep the heck out of me, but Avalon's pretty cute. "And where would you run to?"

I know at once that I've asked the totally wrong question. Avalon's eyes widen and her lip quivers. "Just around the woods," she says. "Or when we needed to go into town, I could run there so fast and we wouldn't need to take a car on that bumpy road."

I force a smile. "That does sound fun. Maybe *I* want eight legs, too."

The others have gone silent. Did they think I meant the question to be more than it was? I figured she'd say something whimsical and childish, like "all the way to space!" or "to see the ocean!" I didn't realize she wasn't even allowed to have an imagination.

Her reaction concerns me. Is she . . . scared of Firehorse? I glance up at Alexa. She looks casual, but . . .

Is Alexa scared of him, too?

Just as I'm about to open my mouth, the man himself appears. "Mailee!" he says, all jovial and bouncy. "I've just spoken with your parents. They wished you'd told them a bit more about where you were going, but they're happy to let you spend the weekend here."

So he couldn't get his range extender thing to work on the ground, but he climbs a tree a little ways and magically has a great conversation with my parents? Who are completely fine with me being gone all weekend with some strange man? This feels really wrong. But Cara looks pleased, and there's nothing I can do about it now.

He falls into step between Alexa and me, so close to her that their fingers brush. It doesn't seem to bother her one bit, and makes me wonder—again—what kind of relationship those two really have. I get that he has no sense of personal space, but they have a comfort level that seems beyond platonic.

"Thank you so much for calling them," I say. "It's such a relief to have them know where I am."

"Of course." Firehorse pats my shoulder. I am quickly growing to hate when he does that. It feels condescending. "Anything I can do to make you more comfortable, Mailee."

He says it in a very sincere tone of voice, but I have a gut feeling it was sarcasm. I'm trying not to anger him, because I'm more and more worried about what incurring his wrath could mean, but it seems like I'm failing anyway.

As the day wears on, I start to wonder if, at some point, my feet will fall off my body. If they'll scream, *"Enough!"* and leap off and refuse to go anywhere ever again. I'm not a total slug or anything; I do exercise. But walking on an uneven forest path for a full day is an entirely different beast. My legs are killing me.

It's so pathetic, but I'm starting to straggle. Cara and her new group of friends are so far ahead of me, I can't even see them. This includes Avalon and her tiny child legs.

Brigit is closer to the back of the group, but Firehorse is hovering near her, so she hasn't looked back at me once. Or maybe she hasn't looked back at me once because she doesn't care that much about my whereabouts. That's entirely possible. I mean, why would she?

I step over a log, and I just can't anymore. The log calls to me. So I stop and sit. Stretch out my legs before me and wince at the ache in my muscles. I want to curl up in a ball and die. Maybe it's dramatic. But that's how I feel.

I have no idea what time it is, so I retrieve my phone from my backpack and turn it on. 4:17. Could be worse, I guess. But

I still have no clue how much longer we'll be walking and I'm so exhausted. I shove the phone back in its pocket, drop my face into my hands, and try not to cry.

"Mailee?" I look up at the sound of Cara's voice. "Firehorse sent me. He said he saw you sit down and he was worried about you."

"I'm fine." I let her pull me to my feet, but very reluctantly. "I am just embarrassingly unprepared for all this hiking."

"Don't worry about it," she says. "My feet hurt, too."

If only that made me feel better.

"Come on." She hooks an arm through mine. "I'll walk with you. At whatever pace you need to go."

"Thank you." I smile at her. This is the Cara I remember.

Except, she's also a Cara who has changed so, so much in the months since she told me she needed space. I realize with a little lurch in my gut that I'm not sure what to say to her anymore when we're not mixed into a group of people. Or when I'm not trying to convince her to get out of here.

"Hey, did you ever get the text I sent you last week?" I ask, trying my best to sound casual.

"Oh, yeah, the one about the play? I meant to reply." Cara smiles broadly. "I'm so proud of you! You've worked really hard; I'm so glad you'll get to be the lead." She pauses, biting her lip. "They announced stage manager this week, right? Who got it?"

It's my turn to hesitate. "Steve."

"That's great. He deserves it." She seems like she wants to say something else, so I wait. Stare at my toes as I step over rocks and roots crossing the path. "I, um . . . did Mr. Ingleton tell you I asked not to be considered?"

I stop walking. "You . . . *what*?"

"Yeah, I, um . . ." She shoves her hands into the front pockets of her jeans. "I mean, I'm part of the Haven now. And I worried that even though I've been kinda patchy with my attendance this fall, they might still assign me stage manager based on my history with drama club, you know? So yeah. I asked not to be considered."

That cuts deep. She openly told me she was planning to live here now, so what did I expect? But I hadn't thought about it, not really. When will we hang out after this? *I'm* not quitting school, and *I'm* not quitting the play, so . . . where does that leave us? Is this trip, like, a good-bye for her? I've been so wrapped up in wondering what Firehorse is planning that I haven't dealt at all with what Cara's up to.

"I'm sure Steve will do a great job," I say, "but you would've done better."

"Of course I would have." Her smile is genuine; she has no idea how sad I am. "But, I don't know. It's just not calling to me anymore. When I think about my future, I don't feel like I want any part of the fakeness of that entire industry."

The fakeness of the entire industry? Awesome. That makes me feel great. "I don't . . . I hope you don't think I won't want to be friends with you if that's not your life goal anymore. There are *lots* of things you could do. You're so smart and organized, you could do anything."

"Thank you for saying that." She swipes a sweaty strand of blonde hair away from her face. "But the thing I want to do, you don't seem exactly . . . one hundred percent supportive."

"You mean . . . this? The commune?"

She nods.

"I'm—it's a lot to swallow. We've been best friends for ten years, and then you came here a couple times and didn't need me anymore."

"It was more than a couple times," she admits. "I came again and stayed for three days while you were at theater camp, and then . . . I went again the day my parents left for their trip, and then for a couple more days after I saw you that week."

"I see. And this fall, you've been . . ."

"I haven't been living here this fall, technically. I've been spending weekends, and evenings when I can, and skipping school sometimes."

Skipping school more than just *sometimes*. "The school hasn't contacted your parents? You've missed, like, a third of the days."

"Mom knows about pretty much all of those days. I told her about breaking up with Jackson, and, um . . . well, she noticed you hadn't been around as much so I told her we were having trouble, and she thinks I'm having panic attacks over it all, so she's been letting me stay home a lot."

"So you're—" Nope. I can't. I shut my mouth. I want to explode about how not-cool it is to pretend to have anxiety symptoms when you don't, and how *terrible* of an idea it is to emotionally manipulate and lie to your mother, besides. But she is finally opening up to me, finally being honest. I need to let it happen without judgment. "So this is really what you want to be doing, and you have no reservations?"

"It is really what I want to be doing."

"And no reservations?" I repeat.

She hesitates. For a long time. "None."

For the first time in my life, I am so happy to hear Cara lie.

NINETEEN

The Cave is . . . a cave. It's not at all what I was picturing. With the capital-C way Firehorse talks about it, I had envisioned some sort of glorious spectacle of nature, but it's just a narrow hole nestled between some rocks. Tall enough I wouldn't have to crouch, but not tall enough that Firehorse wouldn't.

The others don't look too impressed, either, which makes me feel better about the letdown. I don't want to be the only one with outrageous expectations. Brigit stands with a boy and a couple girls, and they all look majorly skeptical. Even Avalon doesn't seem to have a whole lot of enthusiasm about it, and she's enthusiastic about everything.

Firehorse, however, is alive with excitement. He gathers us around the cave—which we are not to go inside of, by the way—and he makes a ridiculous, overwrought speech about how he was hiking around up here and discovered this cave and that's what made him decide to buy the land and start the Haven here, as opposed to anywhere else in the world.

I can practically feel the others thinking the same thing I'm thinking: *Really?* This *cave, of all the caves in the world?*

But he's so into it that it's almost infectious. I'm, like, growing fond of the dumb cave because Firehorse is so overjoyously obsessed with it. This is Firehorse at full power. This exuberant, passionate human being is the one who recruited all these people, who caused others to feel as invested in his cult as he is. This isn't the Firehorse I ever saw, and it makes me all the more certain that he never intended for me to be part of this. He almost sucked me in using only his manipulative little speeches. Imagine what would have happened if I'd gotten a show like *this*.

Goose bumps pucker the flesh on my arms. Beside me, Cara's holding hands with Finn, and it makes me feel very alone. I can't concentrate on what Firehorse is saying; I can only concentrate on Cara.

She looks happy. She's so proud to be part of this. Does she look that happy when we hang out? Or am I an obligation, someone she wanted to see one last time before she cuts me out of her life completely?

I quite literally don't know what I'd do without Cara. If I never see her or talk to her again after this . . . I'll be totally lost. And honestly, even if she decided it was time to leave right this second, from now until forever I'll always know, for sure, that I need her more than she needs me. Because she could walk away from our friendship. She *did*. And I can't. I'll never be able to. It's unthinkable.

I blink back tears. I can't let them fall right now, not while Firehorse is going on dramatically about the gloriousness of the Cave, and nature, and believing in each other. But Cara notices. Of course she does. And when Firehorse is done with his speech, and the group disperses to start setting up the tents, she asks me about it.

"I'm fine," I say, and I pull our tent out of its bag like that somehow proves my okayness.

She doesn't push it, and the tent is halfway put together before I break.

"Am I going to see you again after this?" I ask.

She glares at me around a pole. "What? Of course."

"When?"

She's silent.

"You were fine with me joining the cul—the commune because you knew I'd never do it. Firehorse, too. You didn't invite me to this because you thought I'd join, too, you just wanted to say good-bye. I'm right, aren't I?"

Now her eyes are filled with tears. One drips down onto her cheek. "This was never about leaving you. That's never what I wanted. You've been my best friend for a freaking decade. I didn't forget about that. But joining the Haven means giving up some things. I'm living way out here. I know you won't come visit. So as a byproduct . . . I don't know. Maybe we'll see each other again. I hope so. But I can't count on it."

Her words stab me in the stomach. "I would come visit," I say softly, "but would I be welcome?"

She brushes away the falling tears. "I guess that depends how you act."

The tent's together now. I throw my sleeping bag inside of it and walk away. I can't do this. Can't let her act like it's on me whether or not our friendship survives her move to the Haven.

"I think you should take the Book of Life Goals," she says to my retreating back. I stop but don't turn around. "It should be with you now."

I start walking again, away from Cara, away from this whole camp and the stupid cave, into the trees. I collapse at the base of one, curling my head pathetically against a big root, and I start to cry.

Brigit finds me. She places a tentative hand on my arm.

"Are you okay?" she asks, even though I am very obviously not okay.

"I'm not going to see Cara again," I say miserably. "She's going to stay here, and I'm going to go home, and I'm not going to see her again."

I sit up, with my back against the tree. Brigit sits next to me and scratches shapes into the dirt. "I think . . . it's important that you not give up on Cara right now. Or, more importantly, I guess, don't let her give up on you."

"What do you mean?" I try to wipe my face, but I'm pretty sure all that happens is I smudge dirt all over myself.

"What I mean is . . ." Brigit's eyes dart around, and she continues in a low voice. "I lost my best friend, too. It was here, at the Haven. There was an accident."

My blood chills. The word *accident* echoes in my head, and I think of the trapdoor in the root cellar. "I think Alexa told me about this. Sort of. Just about the, um, the accident. In the root cellar?"

Brigit's mouth twitches down. "Yes. We were all foraging in the woods, and Firehorse sent Opal back to get some tools he'd forgotten. When she hadn't returned a couple hours later, I started to worry, but Firehorse brushed off my concern. Opal could be . . . she got lost in her own world a lot. She would get distracted by an insect or a rock formation and totally forget what she was supposed to be doing. But she was also worried that if she didn't rein that in, she'd have to leave, so she'd been working really hard at adhering to the schedule, listening to instructions."

There's a sound in the underbrush behind us and we both jump—but it's only a chipmunk, darting between the trees.

Brigit takes a shaky breath and goes on, her voice even softer than before. "When we all got back to the Haven a few hours later, she was nowhere to be found. Firehorse still thought everything was fine, but I was *really* worried by then, and Alexa convinced him that we should send a search party out into the woods. While the search party was away, I noticed that the door to the root cellar was wide open. Richelle found her inside, in the freezer. The trapdoor was all clawed up and she was . . ." Brigit's eyes well up and she takes another deep, shaky breath before she can go on. "She was dead. Nothing's been the same for me here, not since then. I started to question things. Not out loud, because I—it was an accident, her death, I'm not saying it wasn't. But the way the whole thing got framed, afterward, like it was her fault for going in the freezer alone, like we couldn't have saved her if we came back when I first told Firehorse I was worried . . ."

"I'm so sorry." I swallow a heavy lump in my throat. I can't even begin to imagine how that must've felt. "I don't know what to say."

"Just don't give up on Cara," she says weakly. "Lately, I've noticed a lot of things that don't quite add up about our little commune. I'm worried about this harvest celebration, Mailee. I'm very, very worried."

"Me too," I whisper, and squeeze her hand. I don't know if it comforts her at all. It doesn't comfort me. "And I won't give up on her."

"There's a reason Firehorse has been trying to keep the two of us apart," Brigit says. "A reason I've only been alone with you in snatches, even though the fact that we've bonded should be a good thing. Normally, he'd be using me to pull you into the fold, you know? But he wants us apart. Which means I'm not doing such a good job anymore, hiding my concerns. So we both need to be very, very—"

We both hear the sound of footsteps, drawing closer. Brigit throws her arms around me and starts stroking my hair, whispering soothing nothings, like this is what she's been doing the whole time. For my part, I try to look like I'm still crying. Like I'm not terrified out of my mind.

"It's time to cook dinner," Firehorse says, looming over us.

Brigit lets go of me, and I try to look pathetic and sad as I get to my feet.

"I'm very sorry if you and Cara had a fight, Mailee," says Firehorse. "And I hope Brigit was able to provide some comfort. But work has to come before emotions, unfortunately."

"I understand," I say shakily. "I'll come help. It's no problem."

Brigit and I exchange a glance as we follow him back to camp. The fear in her eyes is as plain as if she'd tattooed it across her face. My gut twists sickeningly.

She and I, we are in serious, serious trouble.

Cara doesn't talk to me at all during dinner, and when I try to make eye contact as I head back to our tent, she aggressively avoids it. I feel . . . numb. Everything is such a mess that none of it is even getting to me anymore. I don't even bother to look around the tent for spiders before I close my eyes and fall asleep.

My dreams don't provide me with the same sort of numbness, however. They're twisted, disturbed. The kind of dreams you know are dreams, but you're mired in, can't escape from. I'm dreaming about Opal, even though I have no idea what she looks like. In my dream, she's basically Cara, except I know that she's not. She's screaming and clawing and trying to escape. I'm trying to help her, but I can't get my hands to close around the trapdoor's latch. She goes silent, and then—

"There are guns in his tent."

At first I think the words whispered into my ear are part of the dream, but then someone's poking my arm and I realize Cara's trying to wake me.

"What?" I mumble groggily.

"Guns, Mailee."

My brain's working at, like, a quarter strength, so I have to run this sentence through it several times. "In whose tent, Firehorse's?"

Even with only the light from the nearly full moon, I can see her eyes roll. "What would I be doing in Firehorse's tent this time of night? No, Finn's."

I sit up slowly, holding my sleeping bag around me like a blanket. "What kind of guns?"

"I didn't get a great look, but big ones. And I don't want to be, like, alarmist or anything, but they didn't look like rifles. They looked . . . assaultier."

"Assaultier?"

"Oh my God, Mailee, now is not the time to pick on my grammar."

"I know, I'm sorry. What'd you do when you saw them?"

"I pretended not to. They were tucked along the edge of the tent and they were covered up by what I thought was a spare blanket. The edge of the blanket got pulled off a little bit. He put it back immediately and I just . . . I kept on kissing him like everything was the same, like I didn't see. I stayed in there for, like, a half hour afterward so he wouldn't be suspicious."

"Just kissing?"

"Yes! Jeez."

"I know, sorry. I just . . . don't know what to say."

"I think we should tell Firehorse, don't you? He'd want to know that someone brought guns."

Ugh.

"Cara. I feel like . . . I don't want you to get mad when I say this, but I'm pretty sure Firehorse already knows. They're probably there at his instruction."

Cara buries her face in her hands. "I don't think so, Mailee. I—there's no way he knows about this. He's a huge pacifist."

"Is he?" I whisper. If she gets mad, she gets mad. But this is my best and possibly only shot at showing her Firehorse's true colors. "Does it make sense that Finn would have managed to sneak guns up here without anyone noticing? Firehorse notices *everything*."

"No way, Mailee. Just—no." She's trying to talk herself out if it, I can tell. "This is Finn. I should've known. I mean, you told me you got a weird vibe from him the very first time we came, and I ignored you because he was cute and I wanted someone to flirt with after Jackson."

I also told her I got a weird vibe from Firehorse, but she's got no problem ignoring *that*.

"Something's not right in the Haven," she whispers, voice laced with fear. "I've had this feeling about it for a couple weeks now. I think someone's trying to sabotage this commune and before I wasn't sure who it was, but now it's clear that it's Finn."

"I think we can say for sure that Finn is a creep," I agree. "But please, Cara, *please* don't say anything about this to Firehorse. Not until we figure it out more. I think he's—" I cut myself short because I hear the soft shuffle of footsteps drawing nearer. My heart races.

"Cara? Mailee?" It's Firehorse's voice outside our tent. "Is everything fine? Richelle told me she heard frantic whispering."

I unzip the tent partway. "Everything's fine in here. I'm so sorry if we disturbed anyone. Just gossiping about, um, girl stuff."

"Ah, yes. Girl stuff." Firehorse's eyes flick toward Finn's tent. So he knows where Cara came from. Was it Richelle who sent him this way, or was it actually Finn? "You'll need to go to sleep now, okay? Cara's got a big day tomorrow."

"We will, Firehorse, sorry." Cara beams back at him. She is so taken in. What's he going to have to do for her to realize he's creepy? At this point, I feel like he could say it outright and she wouldn't buy it.

He leaves, but even after his footsteps have retreated, I don't dare talk to Cara about this more. Not if Richelle is apparently trying to eavesdrop.

"I guess we should go to sleep," Cara says. "We can . . . figure this out in the morning."

"Yeah." I lay back on my pillow, but sleep doesn't come so easily this time. My worries about bugs crawling on me have returned, and I need to do a check before I can rest peacefully(ish). I feel around until I find my flashlight, and try to click it on. Nothing happens. Have I overused this thing, killed its batteries?

"My flashlight's not working," I say, frowning.

"Good. You'll sleep better if you don't have that thing as a crutch."

I sigh. I miss Cara. Actual Cara, not Condescending Nature Expert Cara. "I'll just turn on my phone for a second. At least it'll be good for something."

I reach into my backpack and dig out my phone. Which, oh crap, I forgot to turn off after I checked the time earlier. The battery's not too drained, though, thank God. I'm at 53%. No service, though. Not that I was expecting it.

But.

I sit up straight. At some point during our travels this afternoon, I *did* have service, at least for a second. I have four text notifications. I open my messages. They're all from Gavin.

Mailee I know something went wrong. You should be back by now and your phone keeps going to voicemail. I'm telling your parents where you are. I hope you're not mad.

I talked to your parents. They said they spoke to Firehorse and you both on the phone and that you and Cara are on

a camping trip with the commune all weekend. That's a lie
isn't it? You didn't talk to them. You're still not picking up
so I know you don't have service. I don't know what to do.
I hope you're ok.

YOU HAVE TO GET OUT OF THERE. I did some research
on Firehorse and it's bad. I hope by some miracle you get
this text. Just get out of there any way you can.
Immediately.

That third text contains a couple images. Screenshots from
an article about a group called Sons of Truth. It features head-
shots of the members, one of whom is Firehorse—his hair is different and he has a beard but it's unmistakably him—with the
name John Merle underneath. I don't recognize any of the
others, just a bunch of middle-aged, generic-looking white guys
with scowls. They're considered a potential threat by the US government, and were thought to have aggressive militaristic plans.

Until they all fell completely off the radar, thought to have
disbanded. The article questions whether they really have, or if
they've just gone underground until the heat is off.

I turn to ice. Are the others coming here? Are they involved
in the Haven somehow, even if I haven't seen them? I'm shaking
as I read Gavin's last text.

I really hope you get these texts, Mailee. I'm telling your
parents what I've found, and I'm telling them I think you

and Cara are in serious danger. Please do whatever you can to keep yourself safe.

My hands quake.

"Cara," I hiss.

She rolls over and looks up at me. "Mailee, we're not supposed to be talking."

"I know." I slide back down into my sleeping bag and move my face close to hers so I can talk as quietly as possible. "But you have to read this."

She takes my phone with a small sigh. In the eerie glow of the screen, I watch her eyes grow wider and wider. "What is he planning?" she whispers, barely audible.

I shake my head. "I think it's bad. Brigit's really worried."

"We have to get out of here."

Finally, she sees what I'm seeing. *Finally.* But I'm worried that now, it might be too late. "Yeah. Like, right now, I think. And we can call someone and get help."

She bites her lip. "What about Avalon? I don't think I can leave her in danger like this. She's only a little kid . . ."

I don't want to leave Avalon, either. Problem is, Firehorse has guns and we don't. And even if we somehow managed to *get* the guns, we don't know how to use them. We also don't know what he's planning. I assume he has no problem killing anyone he perceives as a threat, but he might not be planning to kill those he doesn't. His probably romantic relationship with Alexa might keep her safe. "What are we going to do, though? I think we need to let the police handle this. But first we have to get ourselves out of here."

Cara nods, but I know she wants to warn Alexa. I think of Brigit, who's already scared, and I'm worried for her. For all of them. We can't say anything to Alexa. She'd go straight to Firehorse and that could be dangerous for us all.

"I think it's safer," I say, "if none of them know anything. I hope I'm not wrong about that. He's more likely to hurt the people who know too much."

I can't believe I'm saying these words. Calmly discussing how to escape from someone who could kill us any second.

"You're right." She hands me back my phone, and I shut it off. "We should pretend to be asleep for a couple hours, probably. So no one's up when we go."

"Good idea."

We both burrow back into our sleeping bags, laying quietly and tensely in the darkness. At one point, she whispers, "I'm sorry," but I can't bring myself to reply with the standard, "It's okay."

So I burrow in deeper, and pretend I heard nothing.

TWENTY

There's nothing to do now but run.

We don't take our tent; that'd be like setting off a firework to announce our departure. We only take my smaller pack because we don't want to be burdened and we plan to run out of here as fast as our legs can carry us anyway. We don't need much other than our sleeping bags, both of which I manage to hook onto my pack. I glance toward Brigit's tent, feeling conflicted, but she's sharing it with someone else. I can't trust that her tent-mate wouldn't shout for Firehorse the second we said we were leaving.

Cara and I creep along until we're deeper in the trees. We can't take the path because it's too obvious and Firehorse will find us in ten seconds. And we can't be too close to the path for the same reason. So we're basically guessing at which direction will lead back to civilization and praying to God we're right.

Otherwise, we're both dead.

"I think we can run now," Cara whispers.

And we do. Well, kind of. It's not very easy to run in the forest, what with all the undergrowth and fallen trees and thorns. This is compounded by the fact that it's nighttime. If the moon weren't so near full, I don't think we'd even be able to see well enough to walk. As it is, I keep getting slapped in the face by tree branches, and if I weren't so scared, I would not have the emotional capacity to handle the number of spiderwebs I've passed through. There's little worse in this world than the creepy sensation of those thin strands clinging to your skin.

The terrain is growing hillier, rockier. I hear a thump and a curse word in unison, and stop dead. "Cara?" I whisper. "You okay?"

"I'm fine," she rasps. "I fell. A rock knocked the wind out of me."

I crouch beside the moving shadow I can barely make out as Cara. "I'm not sure we can safely keep going right now."

She inhales sharply, shakily. "You're right. It's getting really steep. And really dark. But the only thing is . . . we don't have any advantage if we don't get a head start."

"I know." I frown. "He could easily catch up to us tomorrow. I have no idea how to cover my tracks or, like, hide in a tree or . . . I don't even know what you're actually supposed to do if you're escaping from someone in the woods."

"We should have watched more horror movies," she says, deadpan.

I laugh, just a little. We've both been boycotting horror movies since my freshman year when a short-lived drama teacher told me my talents were suited for "secondary roles in B horror movies at best." Now even seeing advertisements for horror movies makes me mad, even though I know there are much worse things than landing a secondary part in a B horror movie.

Like this situation I'm in right now.

"Let's try to make it down this hill and then we'll . . . I don't know. Camp?"

"Okay," she agrees, and takes my outstretched arm.

We pick our way down the rocky slope, stopping when we reach a flatter area. We unroll our sleeping bags in a spot where there's a slight outcropping, which makes us feel at least a little bit hidden.

From people, anyway. I hadn't considered other dangers— like bear, wolves, wildcats—until I burrowed, shivering, into the sleeping bag. My breath frosts in front of my face, and I wonder how easily a predator could sense our presence.

Cara, somehow, falls asleep. I don't. Fear and cold make it impossible for me. Nighttime temperatures this time of year are usually in the forties and even huddled inside this sleeping bag, which boasts on its tag that it's good down to twenty degrees, I'm shivering. Spiders are the least of my concerns now. Anything could be out here.

A twig snaps nearby and I hold my breath. A rhythmic scraping sound against the forest floor moves closer and closer to our resting spot. I'm frozen with fear. I can't protect myself against anything. We have literally no weapons. A grizzly bear could rip out my innards with one rake of its claws. I reach slowly for my flashlight, hoping maybe I can at least pound it into the face of whatever's coming near, if I have to.

Scraaape. Crunch. Crunch. CRUNCH CRUNCH SCRAPE CRUNCH.

My heart gets louder as the footsteps get closer. A rounded shadow appears, passing slowly by us. A porcupine. I exhale, slowly. We're okay. As long as it doesn't notice us, we'll be okay.

It stops, maybe five feet from my head. It makes a snuffling sound like it's located something nearby and isn't sure if it should feel threatened. All my instincts scream at me to flee, but that's the worst thing I could do right now. I absolutely do not need porcupine quills lodged in any part of me.

The porcupine shuffles onward, and I can breathe again.

But I can't sleep. Every time the spine of a tree creaks, every gust of wind, every leaf that flutters down startles me like an electric shock. It's agony. The moment the sun starts to rise, I gently shake Cara into consciousness.

"Ugh." She looks around blearily at our surroundings. "I really, really hoped this was all a nightmare."

"Me too." I frown. "But we've gotta get going."

We roll up our sleeping bags, and I shrug the backpack onto my shoulders. She can have a turn later. Now that we're alone, and not within easy listening range of someone else's tent, I tell her Brigit's version of what happened to Opal in the root cellar, the concrete structure I found, everything else that sketches me out about Firehorse and his Colonists.

"I wish you'd told me all of that so much sooner," she says.

"I would have. I tried, remember? I told you about Opal, but you brushed it off. I know that was an accident, but the way Firehorse reacted, like it didn't even matter that she died, it's pretty messed up. You didn't want to hear about it, though. You didn't want to hear any of my concerns, so I just . . . stopped trying."

She holds back the branch of a tree so we can both pass by without it slapping us in the face. "I guess you did try. I should have listened."

We're silent for a long time after that. Hurrying, tripping, clambering through the trees and underbrush. It's hard going. I've twisted both my ankles a little, and one of my knees is starting to hurt pretty bad. I'm scraped up from falling several times, and I want nothing more than to be at home in my bed, sleeping.

"Cara?" I ask tentatively, when I can't stand the silence any longer.

"Yeah?"

"Why'd you invite me to this harvest thing? You barely spoke to me for months and then . . . you invited me and you were so excited for me to come. Was it really just, like, a good-bye thing, or was there something more?"

"I guess . . ." She swallows so loudly I can hear it. "I guess part of me was scared to do it alone. I never dreamed it was Firehorse, but like I told you last night, I had a feeling lately something was off. I didn't want to believe it, but I . . . something in me knew I shouldn't be alone."

I nod. That's something. But I hadn't realized until this moment, I'm actually pretty mad at her for this.

"I'm really sorry, Mailee. I should've—"

"Why, though?" I interrupt furiously. "Why'd you do this? It's so—I know you've been having a hard time, but to turn to a cult? To tell me I'm stifling you and you need space and just . . . you gave up on me, Cara. You completely gave up on me. I would *never* do that to you. Look where I am, for *you*. And you couldn't even be there the day they announced I was lead in the play. I really—I needed you to be there and you weren't."

"Okay," she says. "I guess I deserve that. I messed up. But do you know how hard it is to be your best friend sometimes?"

"Yeah, I know, I get it. I'm messy and I'm flighty and I'm a lot of work. But I've *been* that way, always. If you were getting tired of it . . . I don't know. You could have told me differently. I could've worked on it."

"No, that's not what I mean." She winces as a berry bush catches her with its thorns. "I mean, yeah, sometimes I wish you could fold your own clothes without me mothering you into it, but everything in your life goes so well. Always. You have the best parents. They love you and you eat family dinners together and they don't stifle you but they also aren't so wrapped up in their own crap that they don't notice when you're absent even more than usual. You have a boyfriend who thinks you're, like, all the stars in the sky. You know what you want to do with your life, and you'll probably succeed at it. I don't have any of those things. I'm jealous of you all the time and it's so toxic and so unfair to both of us, because it isn't your fault."

That hits me deep inside. I know my life's been pretty good so far. But it isn't perfect. There's so much I've wanted to talk about with Cara the past few months but couldn't, because she wasn't around. What I'm supposed to do at the end of the year when I leave and Gavin stays. My fear that I'll go to LA and find out I'm actually never going to make it as an actress. The constant, gut-twisting anxiety that I'm not good enough for my best friend, that I don't deserve my life to be so easy, that I deserve more tragedy.

None of that, though, is what I need to say to her right now.

"I know you've had it harder than me these past couple years. I know how bad *I've* felt about Harper, and she wasn't my sister. I haven't known what to do, Cara. I should have done better. I should have done so much better. I wish, though . . . I wish we could have had this conversation at home. That we didn't have to be in this situation to finally be real about how things are going between us."

"I wish that, too." She frowns, blinking back tears. "I would give anything not to have come here, not to have dragged you into this."

"Gavin offered to come with me. I should have let him."

"Maybe. But would he even have made this better?"

"Gavin's pretty laid-back about most things. But the second he saw that concrete structure? He would've *dragged* you out of here if he had to."

Cara stumbles over a root, and I catch her arm.

"Thanks," she says. "And I *do* want you to be happy. I hope you know that. I'm glad that Gavin's so great, I'm glad you're so excited about the play and everything. It was just a really hard summer for me. An especially hard summer. I handled it all wrong."

"We'll just have to make sure we get out of here," I say as she disappears around a tree. "And then we can fix what went wrong. I really, truly believe we can."

Silence. I'm worried I said the wrong thing. And then:

"Mailee." Cara's voice is sheer, rip-the-skin-off-your-face terror. "Come see this."

Whatever it is, I don't think I want to see it. But I think I have to. *Be brave, Mailee*, I tell myself. And I edge around the tree.

The ground at my feet is all churned up. Dark, moist dirt blended with surface detritus. And . . . bones. I feel nauseated. Something was buried here, but not buried too deep. Animals have been here, and they've dug it up. Some of the skeleton's missing, but parts of it are still intact. An arm. Fingers.

A skull with patches of dried skin and wisps of hair still stuck to it.

Oh my God. This is *a person*. A person is buried out here.

My stomach lurches and I dry heave. There's not much of a stench. I'd guess this corpse has been out here a few months.

A rock near the skull confirms my guess. It's got the name *Opal* carved roughly into its surface, with a crudely drawn heart beneath. They buried her, all the way out here, and didn't even bother to do a good job of it. My stomach twists again, this time with sorrow. It feels wrong for a person to be so ill cared for, both in life and in death.

"This is how we're going to end up," I say, panicking. "Cara, if we don't get out of here, we'll be shallow graves in the middle of the woods and no one will ever find us again."

I hook my toes under the arm bone nearest me. I don't know what makes me do it. Something compels me; feels like I need to see more of this body, truly absorb how real this is. I lift my foot up, and the arm lifts, too. There's still some lingering connective tissue, and some scraps of material from whatever she was wearing when she died.

It hits me so hard that if it weren't for Firehorse's negligence, she would be alive right now. This is how little he cares about human life; this is what became of someone who was part of his commune. Someone who hadn't even done anything wrong.

She deserves a real funeral, an actual gravestone in a real graveyard where animals can't dig up her remains, where any family she might have could at least come to mourn. If Cara and I make it out of this alive, I intend to make sure she gets one.

The sound of a foot snapping a branch echoes down from somewhere up the hill. Cara and I look at each other like startled deer for a fleeting moment, and then we're on the run. We're not quiet and we're not graceful; we just sprint.

The fear of someone following you, someone who wants to kill you, it's all-consuming. My brain is a series of panicked exclamation marks, and my limbs tremble and threaten to give out, while I beg them not to fail me right now.

We zigzag through the trees, tumbling downhill, snagging ourselves on branches. A twig slaps me directly in the eye, and I just blink really hard as I continue to run. I can't afford to stop, not if someone's after us.

And then, almost without warning, we're at the Haven.

We both stop, utterly shocked.

"How are we . . . there's no way we should have been able to get back here so fast," says Cara, confused. "Right? There's no way."

"Definitely not. We haven't even touched how long it took us to get to the Cave in the first place. This is . . . I don't know, whatever. Let's just get the hell out of here."

We sprint toward the buildings, to the shack where Cara was living when she stayed here overnight. We need her keys, and then hopefully we can find some way to get her car past mine where it's stuck in the road. Or at the very least, drive a little ways to get us an incremental head start over anyone following.

"My keys are gone," says Cara, pawing through the small structure. "They're not where I left them. They're not here anywhere."

I want to scream. "So he took your keys, too. In case I, like, got to you or whatever."

"Dammit, Mailee, I can't believe I got us into this." She sinks to the ground and grips the sides of her head with clawed hands.

I crouch in front of her and yank her hands away. "Stop it. Don't do the blame thing right now, okay? I knew it felt wrong here, but *this* wrong? How could either of us ever have guessed? Let's just . . . let's go to Firehorse's shack and see if we can find anything that'll help. Otherwise . . ."

Otherwise we're in for a long, long walk.

TWENTY-ONE

Firehorse's shack is basically stripped bare. I mean, there's stuff in it. His bed, some clothes, things like that. But aside from some generic trinkets, his personal effects are gone. We tear through it anyway, driven by adrenaline and desperation.

Drawers, pockets, everything. And we find nothing. Until—

"There's something stuck in here!" Cara exclaims. She's pushed a tall filing cabinet away from the desk that sits next to it, and between, there are a few papers that obviously at some point just got shoved too far aside and slipped down.

It's not keys and it's not a communication device, but maybe it'll be illuminating nonetheless. There are six or seven sheets of paper. She splits them between us, and I scan mine quickly.

The first one is nothing I can make sense of. Some kind of unskilled drawing, labeled with Firehorse's freakishly neat hand-writing. It looks like a map, maybe. I turn it in all directions, but I still can't make sense of it. I set it aside to come back to.

The next page is a printout from some website about electromagnetic fields. Firehorse highlighted portions and wrote disorganized notes in the margins about the government and waves and listening to all our conversations. Paranoid stuff, basically. I touch the necklace he gave me. I still think it's crap. I feel no different and I don't understand how frequencies from a necklace could protect me from other frequencies anyway. It's all hot nonsense.

The third page is torn out of a notebook. More of Firehorse's perfect handwriting. Shorthand notes to himself, obviously, because it's all in little snippets that don't mean anything to me. I return to the map. Hold it far away from my face. Suddenly, it clicks.

"Hey, Cara, come tell me if you think I'm right about this." I set the map on the desk and point with my finger. "So it looks like this is the road leading up the mountain. And this is the commune. And then . . . this is where I'm not so sure. He labeled this 'Cave,' but doesn't it look like it's . . . *really* nearby?"

Cara gazes silently at the map for a long moment. Her finger traces a line out from the cave, one that makes a big, big loop. "Do you think it's possible that the cave is just up that steep hill, but he made the path so confusing that no one knows it's actually this close?"

"That's exactly what I was wondering."

We both go peer out the open door at the hill over by where the road comes in. Honestly, it makes perfect sense. The part alongside the road is basically a cliff. On the side that faces us, it evens out slightly, becomes a treacherous hill. There are too many trees, especially conifers, for anything up top to be visible from down here, even in the dead of winter. It's kind of brilliant.

"I bet he watches them from up there sometimes," I say. "Remember that day we visited? And they were all swimming and relaxing and having a great time, and then Firehorse returned early from his little jaunt in the forest? I bet he was watching and he saw that they weren't doing what they were supposed to, and he decided to intervene."

"I bet you're right." She frowns.

"Anything interesting in yours?" I ask, gesturing to the papers clutched in her fist.

"Not really. A bunch of information on electromagnetic fields. Something about GMOs. And this one's a wedding announcement about some guy—wasn't he one of the ones from that text Gavin sent you?"

I glance at the printout, from some Missouri newspaper's website. It's a totally cliché wedding announcement photo, where the couple gazes lovingly into each other's eyes while bracing themselves against a wooden fence. The face and name of the man do look vaguely familiar. He owns a hardware store now, apparently. And is some kind of "pillar of the community." Which, of course, doesn't mean he's a good guy. But based on the giant *X* Firehorse drew over the whole thing, I'm guessing he's not involved anymore in whatever he and Firehorse were both once part of. I wonder if anyone is. If maybe they all figured out it was one hell of a bad idea. Except Firehorse.

"Yeah, looks like one of the guys. Guess Firehorse is keeping tabs on all his old friends."

Cara shudders. "Let's go, okay? Let's just . . . get out of here. We'll tell the police what we know and let them deal with this."

"I could not be more on board with that plan."

We leave the papers on Firehorse's bed and leave the commune behind us. If we had better knowledge of the area, we'd sneak through the woods a little more, but honestly, we're lucky we didn't get ourselves turned around wrong and die already. So we follow the road out of here.

I really wish we had a car.

And weren't so physically exhausted. We start out jogging, but I get a stitch in my side pretty fast, and after that, we just walk as fast as we can, sweating and panting.

We make it to where my car's still stuck. I think it's even deeper than it was when I left it. Which sucks. Not that I could do anything about it anyway.

"Wow," says Cara. "You *really* got this thing in there."

"Yeah, I know." A terrible thought dawns on me. "Do you think . . . the mud is *really* deep right there? Do you think it was on purpose? I mean, my car's stuck here, no one can get in or out around it, you know?"

"Yeah." Cara frowns. "Wouldn't put anything past Firehorse at this point."

I brush my hand along the door of the car, wishing so badly I could get in and drive away.

"Good news is, I think it's only another couple miles before we start to have cell service," I say.

"That's . . . something." Cara has lost her optimism altogether.

So have I, inside, but I guess that's why I'm the actress.

"We'll get out of here, Cara," I say softly, taking her hand.

"Will you?" says a female voice, just inside the trees.

I whip around and there's Alexa, aiming a pistol at my face.

TWENTY-TWO

My heart stops.

"Alexa," I whisper. "What are you doing?"

"What does it look like I'm doing? I'm stopping you." She clicks off the safety with her thumb. My stomach turns into a knot, painfully tight. If she pulls the trigger right now, I'll be dead so fast, I won't even know it happened.

I'm in such shock that I can't process whatever emotions I'm having about this. But Cara, beside me, is crying.

"Do you know what he's doing, Alexa?" she sobs. "Please let us go. Come *with* us."

"If I didn't know what he was doing, do you think I'd be pointing a gun at someone?" Alexa asks. Her expression is grim, determined. "Listen, I'm sorry. I know what you thought we were, and I know you're not bad people. But sacrifices have to be made sometimes. And unfortunately, it's gotta be you."

"What do you *mean*?" I ask, my voice hoarse. "No one needs to get hurt. What do we need to get hurt for?"

"For people to pay attention." She lifts her chin. Her hand, with the gun, is unwavering. "People aren't paying any attention to how close the world is to the brink of disaster. We're all going to annihilate ourselves. We need to *make* them pay attention."

"By being *even more violent*?" I ask through gritted teeth. The longer the gun points at my face with nothing happening, the less real this feels. It is real, though. I have to remind myself that it's real. I could die.

"Yes. And it needs to come from someone the world isn't expecting."

"But is it?" I start to fold my arms and then decide against it, letting them drop back to my sides. I don't want her to think I'm trying anything. "Firehorse is—"

"Oh, Firehorse isn't responsible for this. At least, not as far as anyone who lives to tell the tale will know."

I swallow hard. So the plan is, I'm not going to live to tell the tale. Got it.

Knowing this makes me feel a little reckless. Cara's still crying beside me. But there are two of us and just one Alexa. If I moved fast, could I—

"Don't even think about it," she hisses, cupping the pistol now with both hands, in a practiced, steady grip.

Guess I was too transparent.

"So what happens now?" I ask boldly.

She doesn't break eye contact with me, but she does slip one hand off the pistol, reaching for something in her pocket. A walkie-talkie of some sort, looks like.

"Firehorse," she says into it. "I've got them. By Mailee's car."

Distant crashing noises tell me someone's coming our way through the trees. My heart sinks into my toes. We were never getting out of here. *Never.* It was foolish to even try.

Firehorse is here, and so are Richelle and Brian, the boy who shared a tent with Finn. I guess I can't be surprised. I shouldn't have been surprised about Alexa, either. But I still feel so betrayed, by all of them. They know Firehorse is a monster, and they're going to let him hurt us anyway.

I guess that makes them monsters, too.

All the kindness has gone out of Firehorse's eyes. His fake, jovial demeanor has been replaced by something sinister. We should have seen through his glamour on day one.

We're surrounded, and Alexa still has that gun—the others probably have them, too—but I keep my chin lifted, my posture defiant. Inside, I am ice shards that've melted into a useless puddle of water, but outside, I don't want anyone to see how scared I am.

"Take Cara back to the Cave," Firehorse says darkly. I don't know which of them he's speaking to, because his eyes haven't left my face. "I'll take care of this one."

"No," Cara whispers. Richelle grabs her hard by the arm. "No, don't—you can't hurt Mailee, you can't hurt her. She shouldn't be here, let her go."

Firehorse's eyes flick to Cara, over my head. A smirk crawls across his face. "It's too late for that, my dear. Much, much too late."

I turn around, try to leap for Cara. Firehorse catches me by the shoulders, his fingers digging bruisingly into my flesh. They can't have her. They can't take her, can't kill her.

"Cara!" I scream, but they're dragging her away, even as she kicks and screams and fights.

Something comes alive in you when there's nothing left to lose. We both know we're headed to our executions. We don't know exactly when or how it'll happen, but we know it'll be soon and it'll be horrible.

I kick Firehorse hard in the shin, and he calls me a word that sets my veins on fire with rage. I try to run, but he catches me by the waist, throws me down. My chin slams into a rock. I taste blood on my tongue, and my vision swims.

He picks me back up by my hair; I stumble to my feet.

"You never believed in me, in anything I had to say," he sneers, like it's an explanation for why this is happening.

I wipe the blood that drips down my chin. "Doesn't sound to me like I'd be any better off if I had."

He smiles, and it's like jumping into a black hole and knowing you're going to fall and fall and fall and nothing will stop it no matter how much you scream. "There are all kinds of ways to die. Some are easier than others."

And then he drags me after him. I don't say anything else because I'm sick with fear. It clogs my throat, turns my blood to sludge. He's dragging me down the path, the one I found when I got here on Friday. No. Oh no.

I dig in my heels, try to fight against him, but he's bigger than me. Stronger. And he's better at this. Still, my fear is a wild thing inside of me. It flips the switch on my rational brain, and it takes over with the animal part, the part that's been wired in there for millennia, the part that let us survive back before we were at the top of the food chain. I have to get away. Have to escape, *have to*.

Firehorse grabs my wrists, wrenches my arms behind my back, and pushes me forward ahead of him. I can't break free no matter how I try. When I kick at him, he lets me fall onto my face, then pulls me back to my feet. I spit dirt and rock.

And now, here we are. Standing in front of the concrete building I saw before. Now I know what it's used for, I guess. Firehorse opens the door, and I look up at his face, twisted with hatred and rage.

"Do you even believe in any of this?" I ask in a small voice.

"I believe in the aspects that matter. I believe in cutting myself off from the poisoned world, and protecting myself from all the ways the government tries to spy on us. Although . . ." He pauses, smirking at my necklace. "Sometimes spying has its merits."

I clutch at the pendant. "So you know this whole thing about protecting yourself from electromagnetic fields with special frequencies is garbage—you just convinced everyone it wasn't so you could get them to wear *tracking* devices?"

"Oh, it isn't garbage at all. No, it's very real. Adding tracking devices doesn't make it any less so."

"Whatever you're planning," I say in my smoothest, coldest voice, "I hope you get caught, and I hope you rot away in prison for the rest of your life."

"One of us will be rotting," he says, chuckling hard at his own joke.

And that's it. Firehorse shoves me roughly inside the concrete cell. I fall to my knees. And when he closes the door behind me, I have only one thought: *I am going to die in here.*

TWENTY-THREE

It's pitch-black. The kind of dark so deep that it feels like a physical force weighing on your eyes. I squeeze them shut and then open them as wide as they'll go, but of course neither of those things helps.

My phone's still in my pocket. I yank it out, fumbling to turn it on. It's my only hope right now. Truly. My hand trembles while I wait for it to power on. It feels like forever. I still have 37% battery, so that's good, I guess. But no Internet connection, and no service.

I shouldn't have bothered to hope. Firehorse is a lot of things, but he sure isn't stupid. He would have made sure his cage was as impenetrable as possible, technology included.

"Please," I say, face pressed against the crack of the door. "Please let me out. I'll do anything you want."

I'm pretty sure he's gone. But either way, no response.

It's dead in here. Sound is muffled; I can't hear anything outside. Not wind or footsteps or anything.

Of course, maybe it's just that there's nothing to hear.

I dig my fingers into the tiny crack between the metal door and the concrete wall, shove my shoulder hard against it. Nothing moves, not the tiniest bit. One of my nails does break, though, painfully. I put the tip of my finger into my mouth and taste blood.

Now I'm starting to panic. There is literally nothing I can do. I am trapped and there's no way out.

I pound hard on the door and let out the longest, most bloodcurdling scream of my life. Nothing happens except that now my throat feels torn to pieces. This is bad. This is so bad.

I sink to the floor, edge back into the corner farthest from the door. Curl up with my phone. I don't want to waste the battery on the wildly improbable chance I'm able to use it later, but I need comfort right now, more than anything.

I open up the pictures I have saved on my phone and scroll through them, and I start to cry. There's a lot of Gavin and me. About twenty from the day we tried to take an attractive picture of us mid-kiss, which is not as easy as it looks. One I took of him while he was doing homework on my bed, his brow furrowed in concentration, dark hair mussed because we'd just been making out. One his dad took of us crouching on either side of a fuzzy, pudgy three-day-old beef calf at his ranch. A triple date we went on with Sam and Margaret and Cara and Jackson. *Tons* of group shots with my other friends. Even a few from when my brother visited this summer. He thinks he's too cool now to take selfies with his little sister, but I managed to get him to hold still for a couple, even if he's scowly. Pictures of

Cara and me, millions of those, too, of course. Making faces at the camera. Putting on makeup. Ridiculous poses. I have more pictures of the two of us by far than I have of me with Gavin. When I go back far enough, there are even some of us with Harper. Those hit me like a fist to the heart.

I hope Cara's okay. We can't both die in this place. I tell myself there's no way that'll happen because the alternative is too dark to even contemplate.

As scared as I was before, it's not until this moment, locked away here in this empty square of concrete, that I truly realize how dangerous of a situation we're in. I should never have agreed to come in the first place. The second I saw this building, I should have high-tailed it back to civilization, called someone to come get me, and told my parents I thought Cara was in danger. If I'd done that, we wouldn't be in this mess now.

Why did I think I could save her all by myself? The moment I set foot in that commune on Friday, I was trapped. And I didn't even know it. Once I became part of this whole event, there was no way Firehorse would ever have let me leave.

I just don't want this slab of concrete to become my tomb.

I have been in here for five hours. Which I know because every so often I turn my phone on and check the time. I'm going to have to stop doing that, though, because I've drained my battery down to 17% and I don't want it to get any lower.

My mind cycles over and over through what I could have done differently. Sometimes it goes all the way back to the mall, to saying *no way* to coming here in the first place. Sometimes I just replay the part where Alexa caught us. Pointed the gun at my face.

Gavin made so many jokes this summer about teaching me to shoot a gun so I could go hunting with him this fall. I laughed it off because nothing about that has ever appealed to me the tiniest bit, but what if I'd let him teach me? I could've taken Alexa's pistol, I would've known what to do with it when I had it in my hands.

Of course, that would mean I was okay with killing a person, and I think it's one thing to wish you could have done it and another to be in that situation and actually pull the trigger.

I feel shaky and weakened. It's probably been ten or twelve hours since I've had anything to drink. It's not that long in the scheme of things. But I don't know when—or if—I'll get water again. My throat feels closed up, my limbs like gel. I keep telling myself over and over and over again that I'm not going to die, but I'm having a hard time believing myself anymore.

Six hours and fourteen minutes, and I'm at 15% battery. I feel like the walls are closing in around me, like the oxygen is leaving the air. Maybe the oxygen *is* leaving the air. Am I exhaling more quickly than the oxygen can leach in from outside? I press my face to the crack in the door and cup my hands around my mouth, trying to force my breath outside.

My chest constricts and I realize it's not that the oxygen is leaving the air, it's that I'm panicking. My lungs feel like limp balloons. I slide back down to the floor and concentrate on breathing like normal. I've been breathing my whole life. It shouldn't be this hard.

Panic turns to despair and I can breathe again but I'm lying facedown on the rough, cold floor and I can't find any reason to move. I try to think about people I love. That's what's supposed to give me courage, isn't it? Otherwise, how come villains in movies are always using superheroes' loved ones as leverage?

I peel myself slowly off the floor and pound on the door with the edge of a balled-up fist. The sound is so muted, I doubt it can even be heard on the other side. Fury rises inside me, twisting and building like a storm. I will not be shut away like this. I will not be killed.

I back up until I hit the wall opposite the door, and from there, launch myself with all my strength at the thick sheet of metal barring me from freedom. My shoulder slams into it with a satisfying *thud*, but then pain explodes down my arm. If someone was *right* nearby just now, maybe they heard. But the odds of that are not so great. I rest my forehead against the cool, smooth metal and let out a long, slow sigh.

It might be time to face how truly and completely I am trapped here.

Nine and a half hours, 11% battery. I'm curled up in a ball in the middle of the floor, shivering and whimpering. I'm not sure if I'm shivering because I'm cold or afraid or stunned. I wrote good-bye notes in the memo app on my phone. One to my parents, one to Gavin, one to Cara. I wanted to do more, but 11% battery feels dangerously low. I have now forbidden myself to turn it back on unless death is truly imminent.

It feels imminent.

But it isn't; not yet.

I have maintained willpower and my phone has stayed off. I have no idea what time it is. It might have been five minutes or five hours since I last checked. Time has no meaning when you are lying on your back, staring into an abyss of blackness from which you cannot escape.

It's surprising how quickly I lost hope. I thought I'd hold on to it longer. For the first few hours, I pounded and screamed a lot. But it's like the blackness in here has siphoned all the energy from my limbs. Now I just feel numb. No one can hear me. No one knows where I am. No one is going to save me.

I close my eyes and fall asleep.

TWENTY-FOUR

Someone is nudging me with their foot.

"She's not dead, is she?" A panicked whisper near my ear.

"I'm alive," I groan. My eyes open slowly. Light comes in from the doorway. The door is open! It's dark out, but after the soul-deadening blackness of my enclosure, the night sky looks bright as the sun.

Standing over me are Finn and Brigit. I sit up, backing fearfully into the corner.

"Nice to see you, too," Finn mutters. "You're welcome for saving you."

"Saving me?" I'm trembling. Brigit holds out a water bottle. I take it because I'm so thirsty and if she's poisoning me . . . well, if they're here to take me to Firehorse, I'm dead anyway. It hurts to see Brigit working with Finn, though. I thought she and I were starting a friendship.

"Yeah, we thought it'd be kind of crappy to just let you die." Finn's sarcasm is not appreciated.

"But Cara saw those guns in your tent. And you shared the tent with Brian. You're not . . . I thought you were one of Firehorse's . . . special pets."

"Well, I'm not. Firehorse said he'd found those guns in your car. He asked me to keep them safe. Should've known there was no way either of you would have assault rifles, but I didn't, and that's that. Look, I don't have time to convince you. We've got to get out of here. I assume he was planning to let you die in here, but if he wasn't, I don't want to be around when he comes to get you."

I don't trust him, but for the moment, I have no choice. I glance at Brigit, hoping for reassurance.

"You can trust him," she says, "at least, I'm pretty sure."

Not exactly the reassurance I craved, but it'll have to do. Brigit holds out a hand to help me up. I take it.

"After you and Cara took off, and Firehorse tore after you with his inner circle, some of us got suspicious. I mean, you know *I* was already suspicious. But . . . more of us."

"Especially since a couple of us who *thought* we were in his inner circle were left behind," Finn says bitterly.

"Right, yeah. And while he was away, we found some information in his tent."

I breathe easier when we're outside of the concrete structure, but barely. We're still completely vulnerable. "Wait." I yank off the necklace. "These have tracking devices in them."

"Of course they do," Brigit says bitterly. She tosses her own necklace into the structure after mine. Scowling, Finn does the same.

"Sorry, I interrupted," I say. "What did you guys find?"

"Stuff that indicates he thinks he can somehow trigger the world into a self-made apocalypse by killing all of us, then shooting at the cops who arrive, whenever they arrive, and escaping and trying it all over again somewhere else. Till it works." Brigit's mouth sets into a hard line. "And I don't know who he's planning to frame for it, but I know I don't want to be the only black girl in the vicinity when it happens."

Can't really blame her.

"What I don't understand," I say, "is what Cara has to do with everything. Why is he so fixated on her, specifically?"

"We were wondering that, too," says Finn. "I wondered from the very beginning. He was obsessed with her right away. He was so pleased with Alexa for finding her."

My heart hurts a little, hearing that. "Is that why you were flirting with Cara? Just using her to figure it out?"

I might need him right now for the safety of the herd or whatever, but that doesn't mean I have to approve of who he is as a person.

"At first, a little," he admits. "But I like her. If we all make it out of here, then . . . this isn't really what we need to talk about right now, though, is it?"

"I guess not. What's our plan? What's happening at the commune?"

"Firehorse has gone completely crazy, is what's happened. I honestly don't know what he's planning to do right now, but you and Cara really messed things up for him. I think he's still going to try to follow through on whatever plan he's got, though."

"People are going to die," I whisper.

Both my companions are grim-faced.

"Yes," says Brigit. "And I don't know what we can do to stop it."

"We have to do something, though," I insist. "I mean, he still has Cara somewhere. And Avalon's just a little kid. We have to get her out of there."

"We got *you* out," says Finn in a small voice. "Some of the others . . . they just fled."

I want to lash out at him, scream that it isn't enough, we have to get Cara, but I know if Cara weren't involved, I would already think they'd been so brave.

"I don't want anyone to die," I say brokenly.

"Neither do we," says Brigit. "But we can't save them ourselves."

She's right. And I have an idea. "Take this." I hand her my phone. "Don't turn it on yet, wait till you're farther down the road and more likely to have service. The battery is at, like, ten percent. I think it's a couple miles along when you'll start to get service. Send a text to Gavin. He's the last person I texted, so he should be easy to find in my messages. Tell him he needs to call the police but also that the police need to be aware of who Firehorse is and what he's planning. The police may very well already be on their way. I don't know. After you text Gavin, you can try calling my parents. Or your own parents. Whoever. Just make sure the cops know he plans to kill people, including them."

"And where are *you* going?" Finn asks.

I glance up at the cliff.

"Mailee. What do you think you're going to be able to do?" Brigit asks. "Please don't do that. It's not a good idea."

"Maybe it's not. But I'm not leaving until Cara does."

They both look at me like I'm completely insane. Maybe I am. But I've never felt so fearless. I've never been good at handling adversity, yet here I am, faced with the worst thing I've experienced by far, and I'm handling it. And I'm going to keep on handling it.

"If you're serious," says Finn, "then you should take this."

He hands me a knife. It's the kind that folds in half, but it's not a tiny one. It could do some real damage if it had to.

"Thanks." I smile weakly. "Now, get going, okay? And stay safe."

"Same to you," says Brigit.

Then they both leave me.

And I'm fine. I turn back to the concrete structure. I wish there was something I could do about it. The bolts in the hinges won't budge, but with my knife, I manage to unscrew the part of the lock attached to the door. I put it in my pocket.

I'll get rid of it before I'm anywhere near Firehorse again, but I want to be farther away from the building first.

I crane my neck to check out the rocky ledge in front of me. From here, it looks pretty high. But I think I can climb it. I'm going to climb it. Firehorse won't be able to see me from this angle. I'll have the element of surprise.

Bravery is intoxicating. I get it now. Once you decide to be brave, once you've set yourself on that path, there's nothing to do but continue.

We have a rock-climbing wall in the gym at my school. I've used it before, all harnessed in. I've made it to the top four times. This is just like that, minus the harness.

That's what I tell myself as I reach for the first handhold. *Don't look down, don't worry about what'll happen if you fall, and everything will be fine.*

The climb turns out to be pretty easy. Lots of places to hold on, none of them too narrow. My arms ache and my head swims from the lack of food in my body, but I make it to the top without incident. Trees grow all the way to the edge here. I am, for the moment, completely protected from view. And I take the opportunity to bury my treasure, the lock piece. Take that, Firehorse.

TWENTY-FIVE

The victorious feeling from my climb starts to fade as I realize I have no idea what to do now. I should've asked Brigit and Finn for more information on where things stand up here before I parted ways with them. Some of the people scattered, they said, but how many? Where'd they go? Which of the ones left are working with Firehorse, and which are terrified and trapped?

It's quiet. Too quiet. I creep through the trees until I see the spot where we camped.

No one's there. Where are they? I hear voices, faintly, so they're somewhere nearby, but it makes me nervous that I don't know. I edge around and duck into the cave to give myself a few minutes to think. Darkness swallows me up almost immediately, because the opening is so narrow. I trip and nearly tumble over something solid and please, *please* let it not be a dead body.

Holding my breath, I crouch, reach out my hand, and feel the ground. It's a backpack or something. Thank God. Quietly as possible, I unzip it and reach inside to see if there's anything useful. I'm hoping for a bigger weapon, and I don't know why, because I wouldn't know how to use this knife to defend myself, let alone anything else. But that's where I am, I guess.

Mostly the pack seems to be filled with clothes, but I do find a flashlight. I debate whether or not to turn it on, and settle for turning it on with my fingers over it, so the light it casts is dim and shadowy. I don't think anyone'll notice from outside the cave. And if anyone's in here, they're dead silent. Which means they already know I'm here, flashlight or not.

It's creepy in here, I can't lie. And I'm pretending that caves aren't the sort of place where you find spiders, because otherwise, I'll lose all bravery. I don't know what I'm looking for as I creep slowly deeper. But I don't have a better plan.

The cave is shallow, it turns out. It tapers off abruptly into nothing, and that makes me suspicious. There's no way Firehorse picked this tiny, random cave for no reason. I realize that being able to see the commune below is a bonus, but it doesn't seem like that's all of it.

I crouch and sweep my flashlight around, looking for clues.

And I find one.

A hole in the cave wall, low to the ground and located under the overhang at the back where it'd be easy to miss. I shine my flashlight into it. Should I go in? I'm not super claustrophobic, but the hole is *very* small. It seems like a pretty big risk.

Screw it.

I lower myself through the hole. It's tight. I think Firehorse could fit, but a bigger man definitely couldn't. My toes hit dirt, and after I'm sure I'll be able to pull myself back out, I let go.

With a sweep of my flashlight, I figure out Firehorse's escape plan. There's a pile of rocks sitting nearby, which he could easily build up over the exit to look like it's nothing. Probably no one will even realize this is here. It's narrow where I'm standing, but it widens out quickly, and it goes far. I'm guessing wherever it comes out, he's got a vehicle waiting for him and whoever he's bringing along.

The problem is, he's obviously planning something awful before he flees.

Part of me wants to stay here. Or to run down this tunnel to its exit. It feels safer, less scary. But I can't do that. I came here for Cara, I stayed for Cara, and I'm not leaving without Cara.

So, with all the bravery I can muster, I drag myself back through the hole. I accidentally drop my flashlight behind me, which means I can't see a thing. I curse under my breath and press myself against the wall, edging toward the entrance. I think, at least. I know I'll get there eventually.

The halo of sunlight that is the cave entrance shimmers before me just as a hand grabs my wrist.

"Got away, did you?" Firehorse. No.

He yanks me roughly out of the cave, nearly pulling my arm from its socket. I grit my teeth so as not to make a sound of pain.

The reason I didn't see anyone before is because they're all on the opposite side of the cave I came up from. Near the steep hill that leads to the commune. It looks like most of the escaped commune members have been rounded up, and they all sit quietly, tied up, with guns trained on them by Firehorse's stupid loyal few.

Cara's here, too, and I'm relieved to see her in one piece. Firehorse shoves me hard toward the group. I stumble and fall. When I scramble to my feet and turn back to him, he's holding an assault rifle. Not aimed at me, but its presence is enough.

"Why Cara?" I ask desperately, because I don't know what else to say. "Why did she have to be part of this? Why did you *have* to have her?"

Firehorse chuckles, and it sends chills crawling up my spine. Like the voice of the devil. "This was never about Cara. You figured out so much. I'm surprised you didn't put that together."

"What was it about, then, if not her?"

Firehorse pinches my chin tightly between his fingers. Bruising my jaw. "*You*, foolish child. I needed *you*. Cara was only bait."

I try not to look at Cara as the world spins around me. "But—"

"Everyone here has something in their lives that makes them tragic in the eyes of the media. Abuse, loss, abandonment. Our news outlets like when killers have tragic backstories. It helps everyone sleep at night, to wrap themselves in the false comfort of it. But you, *you* have had a darling life. Your parents, your sweet little boyfriend, your friends, they would all insist that you would *never* do such a thing as this. And there's nothing in your history to prove them wrong. People won't know what to make of it. They'll be so . . . *distraught*."

"You're insane," I whisper. Inside, I'm panicking. He's right; my family, Gavin, everyone would insist I would never do something like this. Because I *wouldn't*. But would they give up, eventually? How hurt will they be, to think I've killed people? To go through the rest of their lives wondering what they didn't see? I feel sick.

"I'm the sanest person here," he hisses, anger flashing in his eyes. "Anyway, it was kind of you not to go with those fools when they freed you. So convenient that you came right back to me. Not that it would have mattered either way."

His eyes flick to something over my head. I turn, and there are Brigit and Finn, both with their hands tied like the others while Richelle holds a gun to their backs. My heart sinks.

"Yes, I was never going to let them escape. I was never going to let *anyone* escape."

Firehorse strides casually past me. I don't move, because he's still holding that gun, and I know he's not afraid to use it. "I knew you and Brigit would bond," he says. "She's been a thorn in my side for a while, but I thought she might prove useful."

Brigit's eyes shoot lightning at him. He turns to Finn, his mouth twitching into a regretful frown. *"You,"* he says, "I thought I might be able to take with me. It's too bad."

Finn spits in his face. Firehorse backhands him with a violent crack, and I cringe. But Finn doesn't cry out, doesn't do anything. He lets the blood dribble slowly down his chin, and doesn't even try to wipe it away.

Firehorse wheels back to me, smiling like this is the best day of his life. I glance at Cara. She looks terrified. I *am* terrified. But at the same time, there's something truly freeing about knowing you have no way out. I can say or do anything I want at this point; can't make things worse.

"It's too bad I won't be here to see how the police react when they find the girl who did this," says Firehorse, still grinning down at me like a monster. "The girl who shot bullets into their midst, who killed every member of this commune."

"You won't get away with it. People have seen you who aren't here. They'll question what happened to you."

"Oh, don't worry." Firehorse grips me tightly by the arm and brings me over to the fire we built when we all set up camp. There's a burnt-up corpse next to the flames, all crisp and blackened. I can't help it. My stomach heaves, and I double over, puking out whatever's left in me.

My eyes sweep over the group. Only three boys left. Firehorse killed one of the boys to be his unrecognizable body. I notice another burnt corpse nearby, and my gut twists again. This time, though, I manage not to be sick.

"We can't have just one unrecognizable corpse," Firehorse says. "That would be very suspicious."

I almost ask *What about Avalon?* because Gavin certainly will ask that when he reads about all this in the papers. *There was a little girl*, he'll insist. *Where is she?*

But if Firehorse hasn't considered this, I don't want to mention it. If anyone here deserves to be safe, it's Avalon. She's just a child. A scared little girl, cowering by the side of the cave while her mom holds a gun to my best friend's head.

"What exactly is this supposed to accomplish?" I ask.

"Chaos," he says simply. "I'll keep doing this until I've started enough chaos that the world implodes. And when that happens, I will be far, far away, safe from the fallout."

"What, like on a spaceship?" I spit.

"So funny, Mailee." His expression darkens. "You think you're so much better than me, but you just don't *know*. You don't see why I'm doing this. How important it is."

"You're delusional." I shouldn't talk to him like this. He could kill me for it. But he's going to kill me anyway, so what does it matter? "But I'd *love* to hear what makes you think it's important that you kill people. Just exactly what it is you think I *don't know*."

He folds his arms and straightens his spine, trying to look formidable now. He's never looked smaller to me. "People are such monsters. It disgusts me to be part of the same species as all of you. I want you all to see how awful you are. You think you care about each other, you think you want the world to be better, but you don't. You'll all revel in the chaos. I just have to help nudge you in that direction."

His *ego*. My God. He thinks he's capable of spiraling the entire world into an apocalyptic implosion. *By himself.* "You think we're so awful and so beneath you, yet *you're* the one doing the killing."

"Because I *have* to. To prove it. Everything has aligned. The world's anger has reached new heights. No one else is willing to make this sacrifice." He grabs my arm and shoves me to the ground. "It's time, Mailee. Time to harvest what I've sown. Before the police arrive, and they *will* arrive, I need all of you to be dead."

He lifts the assault rifle, clicks off the safety, aims it at my head. Cara screams, and I hear the sound like it's muffled through water. Time has stopped.

I have nothing to lose. If I don't move, Firehorse is going to shoot me in the face. If I *do* move, he's probably still going to shoot me in the face. But he might miss. So I do it. The bravest, dumbest thing I've ever done.

I rise up, grab the gun, and yank hard. His finger manages to twitch on the trigger before I tug it from his grasp, and a bullet flies through the space between my arm and my torso. It embeds itself in the ground with so much force, I feel it vibrate.

My ears ring painfully from the sound of the bullet leaving the chamber. I don't have time to think about how dead I'd be if that bullet hit an inch in either direction. All I know is I now have a better grip on the gun than he does, and suddenly, everything's erupted into chaos. I don't think this is the chaos he wanted, though.

I can see it all in my peripheral vision; Brigit got free, somehow, and now she's freeing the others while Richelle and Brian try to stop them. Alexa cowers back, arms protectively around Avalon, who's screaming with fear. Good.

I fight against Firehorse with everything in me. He's bigger, stronger. But if I let go of this gun, he'll shoot me with it and not think twice. And then he'll start shooting everyone else. Something jolts Firehorse forward, like he's been kicked in the back, and he loses his grip on the gun. I hug it to my chest and roll sideways, clambering to my feet at the sight of Cara holding a piece of firewood in both hands. A piece of firewood that she just used to club Firehorse in the back.

I readjust my grip on the gun, hold it like I've seen in movies with the butt against my shoulder and my finger curled around the trigger, pointing it at Firehorse's torso, standing back far enough that he can't reach me. Everyone goes quiet. Waiting to see what will happen.

"You don't know how to use that," Firehorse hisses.

"You're right, I don't. But you already took off the safety, and I know this is the kind of gun that would shoot a hole straight through you, so I don't even have to be accurate. I just have to hit you anywhere."

"You would be willing to kill a person?" He tilts his head to the side condescendingly.

Nope. Ninety-nine percent sure there's no way I could actually pull this trigger and end a life. Even the life of someone as vile as Firehorse. "Do you want to find out?"

He comes at me. I can't make myself shoot him, so I do the next best thing: I throw the gun over the ledge.

He lunges for another weapon, but I tackle him, and so does Cara. I pound at him with elbows and fists and ignore what's going on all around us. Firehorse has hurt enough people. He doesn't get to hurt anyone else. I fight and claw, even as he fights back, punching me so hard in the throat that I can't breathe for a few endless seconds.

Finn joins the fray, throwing his heavier body on top of Firehorse. He grabs Firehorse's hands and holds them together while another girl winds rope around them.

"Ankles, too," I say, holding on to his feet the best I can while he kicks viciously. Cara helps, and the girl winds rope from his ankles to halfway up his calves.

And just like that, Firehorse isn't the one with the power anymore.

Richelle and Brian both still have guns, but so do some of the other cult members now. And they're on my side. I'm pretty sure.

"Kill them, fools!" Firehorse roars, lifting his head to look at Richelle.

She hesitates. I want to duck behind Finn, but at this point, that'd be beyond cowardly.

"Or you could just go," I say. "The three of you could take Avalon, go through that passageway in the cave, get out of here and be safe."

"They would *never* abandon me," Firehorse snarls.

But I think he's wrong. Alexa glances at Richelle, and then back at her crying, quaking daughter.

"We'll let you leave," I say, and I hope it's true. I'm not the one holding a weapon, and I'm certainly not in charge here. But everyone was here for an off-grid vegan hippie commune. I can't imagine they want violence if it isn't necessary.

"Let's go," Alexa says, her voice firm and authoritative. "Richelle, Brian, let's go."

"Alexa!" Firehorse's voice is different now, desperate. "Don't—you wouldn't leave me. We need each other. You know that."

But Avalon's still weeping, nestled into Alexa's side.

"It's over," Alexa says. "This was always about Avalon. You knew it was. I'm sorry, Firehorse. I thought you could keep us safe, but you can't, so I'm done. I'm gone."

If she were speaking to anyone other than Firehorse, I'd feel pretty bad. Her voice is hard, cold. Her face utterly emotionless. But Firehorse deserves this. He deserved to be used by her, to be abandoned when he needed someone most.

"Leave the guns," Cara says, because Richelle and Brian still haven't dropped their weapons as they edge toward the cave.

Brigit aims a pistol at them, and they both set down their guns at once, raising their hands like caught criminals and backing after Alexa, disappearing into the cave. Brigit turns to me, frowning. "Should we have let them go?" she asks.

"I don't know. Maybe we should have a couple people near the cave entrance just in case they come back? Who thinks they could shoot someone if they had to?"

"I could," Finn says, his voice hard. A couple of the girls volunteer, too, and the three of them stand sentry in front of the cave, armed and ready.

I crouch beside Firehorse and grace him with a big, nasty smile.

"Was this the chaos you were hoping for?" I ask.

He turns his face away from me and says nothing at all.

TWENTY-SIX

The real chaos happens when the police arrive. Everyone who's armed drops their weapons the second they show up, and through our sobbing, terrified stories, it becomes clear right away who the criminal is here.

Plus, when I tell them Firehorse's real name, from the article Gavin sent me, they recognize it at once. Seems like they're pretty happy to have caught him. I also make sure they know about the opening at the back of the cave, because the only person in that passageway who deserves to get off free is Avalon.

They talk to all of us, ask millions of questions, and it feels like forever until we're finally allowed to leave. My car was towed out of its mud pit, but I ride back to civilization in the back of a police cruiser, just like everyone else. Cara's with me; we insisted that we not be separated, even though we're all going to the same place.

My parents are already at the police station when we arrive, and so are Cara's. Cara seems surprised, and watching her mother hug her like she never wants to let go is, more than anything, what bursts me into tears. My parents gather me into their arms, and I just cry and apologize and cry some more.

All the fear I held inside of me while I was trying to be brave earlier, it flows out like water you try to hold in your fist. But I'm proud of myself, too. Proud of everyone here, because we saved our own lives, and we stopped Firehorse from doing this not only to us, but to whoever else he planned to attack along his way.

His toxic ideas, his manipulations, all of it is going behind bars along with him, and the world will be better for it. No part of me believes he could have instigated an apocalypse like he wanted, but I do think he would've tried like hell.

"It wasn't you we spoke to on the phone this weekend, was it?" Mom asks, when the flow of my tears starts to diminish. "Your voice sounded wrong, but I thought it was the reception."

I shake my head.

"We're so sorry," says Dad. "We should have listened to Gavin sooner. He was so worried."

"I should have told you where I was going. He shouldn't have been the only one who knew. I should have told you everything about it, and maybe we could have stopped this sooner."

Maybe no one would have had to die. I wasn't close with either of the ones who were burnt up, but that doesn't make me less sad about their deaths. They didn't deserve this. They were just people. All they wanted was a place to belong, and that's not a bad thing.

Brigit hovers awkwardly in a corner, and I leave my parents' side to talk to her. Except, when I reach her, I have no idea what to say.

"Thank you for getting me out of that concrete prison," I say.

She smiles faintly. "I guess it turns out you were going to be freed with or without us."

"True, but still. You didn't have to, and I appreciate that you did." I pause, shoving my hands into my front pockets. "I don't know if you have someplace to go back to or what, but if you need somewhere to stay while you figure things out, I'm pretty sure my parents wouldn't mind."

"Thanks. I might have to take you up on that."

Impulsively, I give her a hug, because she was such a good friend to me over this horrible nightmare of a weekend. I can't believe it was only Friday when this all started. Feels like forever.

But I don't get to do or say anything else, because the police want more statements, and they whisk us away, separately. I'm exhausted when it's over. They warn me that Firehorse will most likely have a trial, and I'll have to rehash all of this. But I don't mind. Anything to put him behind bars. Hopefully, forever.

Cara's family and my family leave the police station together, and we take Brigit with us. I wish I could bring everyone to my house, let them all camp out in the living room or something, but that's probably too much to ask of my parents. I don't know where they'll all go, but wherever it is, it's better than with Firehorse.

As I'm getting in the car, though, I pause. And when I turn my head, I see that Cara's paused, too, getting into her parents' car. We run to each other, hugging tight.

"I will *never* try to cut you out of my life again," she says, voice strained with tears.

"And I will never let you join another cult." I'm trying to lighten the mood. It doesn't really work. "I love you. I'm glad you're safe."

"I love you, too." She hugs me even tighter. "And boy do we have a story to tell everyone at school."

That lightens the mood. I laugh. "We most definitely do."

After:
Spring

TWENTY-SEVEN

Here's the thing about being nearly killed in a cult situation that makes national headlines: It's really great college application material. You can use it for pretty much any essay prompt they throw at you.

All my efforts have started to pay off; acceptances are trickling in. Rejections, too, but let's not dwell on that. Today's the big one, though. Today's the day I can check online to see if I got into UCLA. It's where I most badly want to go.

Cara and I sit cross-legged on my bed, facing each other, laptops on our knees.

"Ready?" I ask.

"No."

"Me neither."

"Okay, well, we have to look, so let's just do it."

"On three."

We count together and both click the link. But when the page starts to load, I can't look. I shut my eyes on instinct.

"I got in," Cara says, disbelievingly. "Mailee, you—Mailee! Open your eyes."

I do it. Scan the page, and—"I got in, too."

I cannot feel my limbs right now.

"So we're both in." A huge grin spreads across Cara's face. "So . . . we're going to California?"

"I guess we are."

We shriek and hug, letting the laptops fall off to the side with no regard for their safety.

Cara didn't apply to schools for film production like we planned in the Book of Life Goals. Instead, she applied to be a psychology major, and she thinks she'd ultimately like to get a master's degree in social work.

"It feels right," she said when she filled out the application. "More right than anything's felt in a long time."

And then she happily crossed out the rest of her plan in the Book of Life Goals.

It's funny, really. The messy, chaotic girl is sticking hard to her original, well-drawn plan, while the organized one forges a new and unknown path. I'm proud of her. We both started going to therapy after what happened to us this fall, and Cara's on medication now for her depression. A depression all of us should have seen and none of us did. Things aren't perfect yet; medication helps but it isn't magic. Still, she's doing so much better these days. It's made me realize how long she's actually been struggling. And how much more I wish I'd done to help.

"You should text Gavin," she says. "He's going to be so happy for you."

I bite my lip. "I will, later."

Gavin's going to a local community college so that he can live and work on his parents' ranch while he gets his degree. It's a topic we're still avoiding, mostly. The subject of how we're going to make this work when our life paths are going down two different forks. The idea of us breaking up makes me sick to my stomach, but I can't see a future where we end up together. You never know, though. If I've learned anything over the past year, it's that you cannot predict what life will throw at you.

Dad knocks on the door of my bedroom, then opens it. "It's on," he says simply.

My gut folds into a snarl. This is it, then. It's time. Cara and I exchange a glance, and take a deep breath almost in unison.

Firehorse's trial has been going on for what feels like an eternity, and today is the day that we get to hear a verdict. The evidence against him seems insurmountable, but the news is constantly reporting stories of men who get away with things. You can't ever be sure, no matter how strongly the odds should be in your favor. I'm terrified. Especially since I testified against him, and the idea of him walking free . . . I would never sleep again, even if I'm all the way in California.

Cara and I join my parents in the living room. The atmosphere is tense as we wait, watching the newscasters speculate about the verdict that's probably being read inside the courtroom as they speak. The media coverage for this has been insane. It makes me happy, to be honest, even though dealing with all the attention while I try to also deal with my emotions about what happened hasn't been easy, because I know how much Firehorse would hate it. He's the one who said he wanted his name to be remembered, and he's the one who said he was ready to harvest what he'd sown. This just isn't the harvesting he planned.

I want to tell my parents about UCLA, but now's not the time. They have no mental space for anything but this verdict, I can see it in the way my mom's forehead is furrowed and my dad leans forward like if he's not closer to the TV he'll miss the announcement.

I reach for Cara's hand and squeeze it tight. She graces me with a tiny smile. Our friendship isn't the same as it once was. It'll never be quite the same again, because we're not the same people anymore. But in a way, I think we're closer than ever. We're certainly much more honest.

The newscaster pauses her monologue, listening intently to something. I hone in on the TV like suddenly my eyes have turned into magnifying glasses. I don't even hear the words she says, all I see is *guilty on all counts* scrolling across the bottom.

Relief floods through me.

He won't be sentenced yet, but I've researched all of these charges—the first-degree murder charges alone would put him away for more than a lifetime, and he's got a lengthy list beyond that. A list that grew and grew once Alexa agreed to talk in exchange for a reduced sentence for her own crimes.

My phone alerts me to a text. It's Brigit: Did you see???

I quickly type back: Yesssss thank God :)

I think about how relieved Brigit must be, too. She stayed with us for a couple months while she got a job and saved for an apartment, and now she's looking into going back to college. And I think about the others, too. Little Avalon, living with her grandparents, who talks to Cara on the phone once a week. Finn, who kept in touch for a while, but went east somewhere and has been busy in his new life.

And then I start to cry. Cara wraps her arms around me, and she's crying, too. I didn't realize how much this had been weighing on me, thinking about what would happen to us if he somehow got off. We're all still picking up the pieces of our lives, and I can't imagine spending the rest of mine looking over my shoulder, waiting for Firehorse to appear and take me out for ruining his well-laid plans.

More arms encircle us; my parents are both crying now, too.

I try to pull myself together because this is a *happy* occasion, and I don't want to feel sad. I concentrate on my breathing until it's under control again, and then I say, "Would now be a good time to tell you Cara and I both got into UCLA?"

"Mailee!" Mom hugs me even harder; I can barely breathe, but now she's laughing and all of us are laughing, and we've stopped remembering the terrible thing that happened and moved on to the good thing in my future.

"I think all this good news calls for a serious celebration," Dad says, wiping discreetly at his eyes like we don't know he was crying along with the rest of us. "Ice cream, girls?"

Cara and I exchange a smile, and then she says, "Ice cream would be perfect."

ACKNOWLEDGMENTS

So much gratitude goes to my editor, Amanda Maciel, for this book's very existence, and for helping me to make it the best it could be. Your enthusiasm and insightful comments have been everything, and I'm grateful we got to work together. Thank you, also, to everyone else at Scholastic who helped this book come together into a beautiful final product!

I am forever thankful for my wonderful agent, Sarah LaPolla. You are the best advocate I could ask for, and I appreciate everything you've done for me.

I would be nowhere without the ladies of YA Highway and my fellow hags. Thank you all, always, for your friendship and support and encouragement. Extra thanks to Kate Hart for being an excellent listening ear while I worked on this book.

Farming and food comes up a lot in this book, so I feel like I would be remiss if I didn't thank all the farmers out there. You are underappreciated, but I know how hard you work and I am grateful for every one of you.

I am lucky to have an incredibly wonderful family: Denis and Jeanne Ward (the best parents), Jackie Ward (the best sister),

Tyler Gaouette, Abel Gaouette, Elaine Millett, Andrea, Roger, and Maren Marecaux. I love all of you immensely.

Extra thanks to my husband, Brandon Millett, and my son, Michael Millett, for living with a writer. I love you both beyond words.

And finally, thank *you*, the person reading this book. I appreciate you most of all!